W9-AJT-708

AN AVALON ROMANCE

SUMMER FLAMES
Ilsa Mayr

After finishing her training, arson investigator Karin Bergstrom takes a job with a new investigative unit which, unbeknownst to her, is headed by her former mentor, Aaron Knight. Aaron had been more than her mentor. He and Karin had been unable to hide their growing feelings for one another. But then a ceiling collapse changed Aaron's life forever and ended his relationship with Karin. To bind a healthy young woman to a man who might never walk again seemed unconscionable to Aaron.

Now, thrown together by fate, can they keep their shared past from interfering with the daunting task of catching an ingenious arsonist? The long, hot summer tests their talents, their loyalties, and ultimately, their love.

SUMMER
FLAMES

•

Ilsa Mayr

AVALON BOOKS
NEW YORK

Published by Thomas Bouregy & Co., Inc.
160 Madison Avenue, New York, NY 10016

Library of Congress Cataloging-in-Publication Data

Mayr, Ilsa.
Summer flames / Ilsa Mayr.
p. cm.
ISBN 978-0-8034-9845-7 (hardcover : acid-free paper)
I. Single women—Fiction. 2. Arson investigation—Fiction.
3. Chicago (Ill.)—Fiction. I. Title.

PS3613.A97886 2007
813'.6—dc22
2007011966

PRINTED IN THE UNITED STATES OF AMERICA
ON ACID-FREE PAPER
BY HADDON CRAFTSMEN, BLOOMSBURG, PENNSYLVANIA

This book is dedicated to the members of the Northwest Indiana RWA Chapter. Thanks, ladies, for your support and encouragement.

Chapter One

If there was anything more stressful than interviewing for a job, Karin Bergstrom had yet to encounter it.

Not even careening down State Street en route to her first major fire as a probationer had been this nerve-racking. Karin checked the address Battalion Chief Edwards had given her. Then she glanced at the building in front of her. The home of the recently formed Chicago South Side Arson Investigation Division could only be described as prison ugly.

She had worked too long and too hard to become one of the city's handful of female arson investigators to let this opportunity slip by.

She *had* to get this job.

If she didn't, her name would be added to the long list of those who'd lost their jobs in the city's latest budget crunch. She would be out of the fire department for a long time. Maybe forever. As scientific methods were developed, arson investigating techniques changed. How long would it be before her skills became outdated?

She *would* get this job.

With determined steps Karin entered the lobby where the directory sent her to the second floor.

Pausing before the arson department's door, Karin smoothed the skirt of her new linen suit. Uneasily, she wondered again if its turquoise color wasn't too bright. Ordinarily she wore neutral shades, having convinced herself years ago that they were more flattering to her five foot ten, muscular frame. This time, though, Karin had let her roommate persuade her that the hot turquoise was perfect for her Nordic coloring. Perhaps Alice was right. She was, after all, a high school art teacher who knew all about color. Checking to be sure that not a single, flaxen-blond hair had escaped its tightly coiled French twist, Karin moistened her lips and opened the door.

The receptionist, a friendly-eyed woman in her sixties whose gray hair hugged her small head like a swim cap, looked familiar. It took only a second before Karin placed her. Mrs. McKenzie had been Aaron Knight's secretary at the academy when Karin had been a student there. As always, Aaron's name evoked the familiar mixture of pain and regret. Quickly suppressing the disquieting emotions, Karin addressed the woman.

"I'm Karin Bergstrom. Chief Edwards sent me."

"I remember you," Mrs. McKenzie said with a welcoming smile. "You graduated from the academy. What can I do for you?"

A little bewildered, Karin repeated, "Battalion Chief Edwards sent me." When Mrs. McKenzie's face showed no sign of knowing what Karin was talking about, she asked, "Hasn't he phoned? The chief hired me as the director's new assistant, pending the director's approval, of course."

For a second the well-trained receptionist's composure slipped. Her eyes rounded, revealing her shock at the announcement. "You're the new assistant?"

"Yes."

"Oh, boy. Is that going to cause an explosion. You're a woman!"

Hearing the dismay in Mrs. McKenzie's voice, Karin's courage slipped a notch. "You mean the chief hasn't told the director about me?"

"Not that I know of." When the receptionist saw Karin's stunned reaction, she added kindly, "But maybe Aaron just didn't get around to telling me about it."

Aaron? It couldn't be, Karin thought, her heart jumping into her throat. The whole situation was assuming a nightmarish quality.

"Excuse me," Karin said, her voice hoarse, "I just realized I never caught the director's name."

"Why, it's Aaron Knight. You must remember him. He was the head instructor at the academy—"

Karin saw Mrs. McKenzie's lips move, but she didn't hear a single word. All she heard vibrating in her head was "Aaron Knight. Aaron Knight." She had trouble breathing as if she had just inhaled a lungful of black smoke. Fighting blind panic with a couple of deep breaths, she managed to speak.

"You did say Aaron Knight, didn't you?"

"Yes. Is something wrong?"

Wrong? Oh, yes. Everything was wrong. Terribly, dreadfully wrong.

"Don't let Aaron scare you. I know he can be a little intimidating. And impatient with people who're incompetent. But you were a good student. Graduated at the top of your class. You shouldn't have any trouble with 'The Iron Knight'. Oh, I know that's what you students called him behind his back," Mrs. McKenzie confided with a wink.

Karin wasn't scared of Aaron. At least not in the way Mrs. McKenzie thought she might be. Her reasons for fearing to see him were vastly different.

When the first shock of discovery lessened, Karin asked, "Did you say Mr. Knight doesn't want a woman for this job?"

"Yes."

That smacked of gender discrimination, Karin thought, anger surfacing. If Aaron thought he could pull that, he could just think again. Before Karin could formulate a strategy, the sound of a door opening claimed her attention.

Aaron.

Karin bit her lower lip till the pain drove tears to her eyes. She had tried to envision Aaron in a wheelchair, but her imagination hadn't prepared her for that heart-breaking sight. A big, muscular man of six foot three or so, Aaron dominated the mechanized chair, making the sturdy metal contraption look flimsy.

She closed her eyes, fighting the compassion that filled her heart. And the guilt that ravaged her soul. Dear heaven above, she'd thought she'd succeeded in convincing herself that she'd had nothing to do with precipitating his accident. Technically she hadn't. The burning ceiling that had collapsed on Aaron had done so because of the fire. And yet, if she hadn't picked that fight before he was called away, he might have been more alert, might have recognized the danger sooner. How often had she read the report of the accident and not once had she found any reason to blame herself. Still. . . .

With steely determination, she pulled herself together.

Thank God she'd caught sight of him before he saw her. It gave her a chance to wipe the shock and the pity off her face. When Aaron saw her, the wheelchair screeched to a halt. In that first unguarded split second, Karin thought she saw joy leap into his eyes before shock took its place. He shuttered his gaze. When he looked at her again, his hazel eyes appraised her face, lingering for a moment on her mouth in a way that told her he remembered their kisses. Karin felt a wave of heat suffuse her skin.

Aaron inclined his head in a silent greeting before he wheeled himself toward his receptionist's desk. He looked at the sheaf of messages Mrs. McKenzie handed him before he glanced at Karin again. Quickly he looked away from her.

Pull yourself together, Knight. Aaron flipped through the message slips without seeing them to give himself time to collect his wits. Dumbfounded, he noted that his fingers were unsteady. He hadn't dreamed that coming face to face with Karin would cause his hands to shake like leaves in a summer breeze.

Twenty-two months had passed since he had seen her. That should have been enough time to prepare himself for the possibility of meeting her unexpectedly. Why hadn't he prepared himself for that? Because it has been easier to tell himself he would never see her again.

Coward. On some level of awareness he had to have known that he would run into her some day. Although Chicago was a big city, the community of arson investigators was small. Calling on his formidable control, Aaron willed his hands to stop trembling. Carefully he aligned the edges of the slips before he addressed her.

"What can I do for you, Karin Bergstrom?"

She had always loved the way he said her name. She still did.

"Chief Edwards sent Ms. Bergstrom." Mrs. McKenzie paused for a beat before she continued. "She's a candidate for the position as your assistant."

Aaron looked as if he'd been poleaxed, Karin thought, dismayed.

"What? That's got to be a mistake."

Aaron shot her a slit-eyed look that made Karin long for the floor to open. Blast the chief. He'd known of Aaron's request for a male assistant, so why had he sent her?

"I didn't ask for a woman. In fact, I specified that I needed a male assistant. This will never work."

"Now just a minute," Karin said, her voice angry. Crossing the space separating them, she confronted him. "Not hiring me because I'm a woman is gender discrimination. In case you've forgotten, that's illegal."

"I haven't forgotten a thing."

Aaron's voice, rich with undercurrents, imbued that simple statement with scores of possible meanings. Karin couldn't even begin to narrow them down.

"Get the chief on the phone, Molly. I don't care where he is or what he's doing," Aaron snapped, his voice like black thunder. He wheeled himself rapidly into his office and slammed the door behind him.

The sound caused Karin to flinch. Aaron was furious and quite determined to get rid of her. This was the worst of all possible beginnings.

Her whole body tensed with anxiety. Uneasily, Karin

glanced at Mrs. McKenzie who, apparently used to Aaron's outbursts, calmly dialed the chief's number. Karin felt no pity for the man who was about to face Aaron's wrath and disapproval. She'd had to do this in her entire career. But this was Aaron, and she and Aaron shared a past. Why did the past always come back to haunt a person? Perhaps she should just walk away. Walk out that door and never face Aaron again.

"Karin? Are you all right? You look a little pale." Mrs. McKenzie rushed from behind her desk. "This heat wave we're having is getting to everybody. Come, have a seat." She touched Karin's arm, pointing her in the direction of a visitor's chair. "I'll get you a glass of water."

"Thank you." Karin managed a wan smile before she sank into the deep armchair.

This couldn't be happening to her, Karin thought, her pulse pounding in her temples like a triphammer. Desperately, she looked around. Before she could push herself from the depths of the chair, the receptionist was bearing down on her, carrying a glass.

"Drink this," Mrs. McKenzie said in her best maternal tone which brooked no disobedience.

Karin drank the water.

"Good," Mrs. McKenzie praised when Karin handed her the empty glass. "Now lean back and relax."

Karin obeyed since she wasn't certain her trembling legs would carry her out of the room. Besides, running away wasn't the answer. She had run once, and that had been a huge mistake, a mistake she'd regretted bitterly ever since.

She tried to relax, but each minute she waited increased her uncertainty, her nervousness, just as it had the first time she'd waited for Aaron. The entire class had been filled with tension and nervous anticipation. Aaron's reputation as a near-legendary arson investigator and as a tough-as-nails teacher had preceded him. As had his reputation with women. It had been lucky that he hadn't looked at her when he'd entered the classroom for Karin was certain her mouth had dropped open. He'd been even more impressive in person than she'd imagined him. When their eyes met for a split second, something had happened to Karin. To this day, she couldn't rationally explain her reaction. Only that she'd felt as if she knew at last why she'd been born.

Dumb, real dumb, Karin. It had probably been nothing more than a physical attraction. A very potent physical attraction. It was foolish to ascribe anything special to that natural, even common, occurrence.

Taking a deep, calming breath, Karin considered her predicament. If she didn't fight for this job, or if she declined the position should Aaron approve her for it, she would forfeit her chances of being rehired when the budget crunch was over. Refusal was tantamount to professional suicide. Was she ready to relocate or retrain for another job simply because she found the idea of facing Aaron Knight painful and difficult? Was she ready to throw away those grueling months at the academy and the seemingly endless first weeks at the fire station where her male colleagues had done their best to drive her out?

No, by heaven, she wasn't.

She wanted this job. She was qualified for it. Yet knowing Aaron, he would make her fight for it. So be it. Straightening her shoulders, Karin sat up tall in the chair.

A good ten minutes later Aaron buzzed Mrs. McKenzie to show Karin into his office. He was studying a bunch of photos on his desk, pointedly ignoring her for several seconds. Without looking up, he ordered, "Have a seat."

Karin sat on the edge of the visitor's chair and waited. And waited. Aaron was punishing her, which meant that his talk with the chief hadn't gone well. Perhaps she still had a chance at the job. If she could handle it. Not the job. That she could perform without question, but could she handle being around Aaron? Could she face seeing him daily in that wheelchair, unable to keep from wondering if in part she was to blame for him being in it? She repressed that thought with a shudder.

Perhaps Aaron was only testing her to see how she would react to a difficult situation. Well, she would pass this test with flying colors the way she had passed his tests at the academy. Leaning back in the chair, she studied him surreptitiously.

Her first impression had been that Aaron hadn't changed at all. Now she saw that she'd been wrong. There were lines around his sexy mouth that hadn't been there before, lines that spoke of pain endured and hopes crushed. Quickly, she lowered her eyes and suppressed the compassion that rose in her, reminding herself that she had to remain unemotional and objective. That was the only way she could survive as his assistant. If she became his assistant. When she felt in control again, she continued her examination of his face.

His nose was as narrow and aristocratic as she remembered. Undoubtedly he was still very good at looking down its elegant length at people, she thought. His mouth. . . . Quickly she raised her eyes to his dark brown hair with its tendency to rise into unruly waves. Now it was still tamed smoothly against his head from his recent shower.

She could remember how it had tangled into wet ringlets after they'd spent hours sifting through the ashes of a factory fire. In an unprecedented move, Aaron had asked her to accompany him on an arson investigation the week before graduation. They had celebrated its successful completion by passing a can of icy cold root beer back and forth, neither bothering to wipe the spot where their mouths fastened onto the can. Even now, she clearly recalled the exquisite pleasure she'd felt touching the metal he'd touched with his lips. That night she'd gone to bed filled with sweet dreams and heady expectations for the future. A few months later, a burning ceiling had destroyed both.

"What do you make of this?" Aaron asked at last, holding out a photo to her.

Another test, she thought. He had always favored impromptu quizzes. Karin rose to take the picture. She examined it carefully before she held out her hand for the others. Aaron passed them to her one by one. Karin took her time. When she was done, she stacked them neatly and handed them back.

"I can't give you an answer because there's something missing, something important. Is this one of those trick questions you used to throw out in class?"

Fleetingly Aaron's mouth quirked as if he were suppressing a smile. Then it settled into an uncompromising, hard line again. "I wish it was." He stared down at the stack thoughtfully.

Karin waited for him to explain. Finally she demanded, "Are you going to make me waste an entire afternoon waiting to find out what you decided about me?"

"Karin Bergstrom, I decided about you a long time ago."

She tried to capture the inflection of his voice, but whatever she thought she'd heard was elusive, leaving her uncertain how to interpret his cryptic statement. Since he didn't seem inclined to elaborate, she asked, "What did Chief Edwards say?"

Aaron looked at her then, his face expressionless. "He said since I trained you myself, I can hardly dismiss you as incompetent as I did the other candidates he sent. I had to agree with him on that."

"Well, thank you."

Aaron heard the flip note in her voice and recalled that she'd been the one student who hadn't been intimidated by him. He'd liked that about her. Among other things. Many other things.

"And?" she prompted.

"And since you're the applicant best qualified for the job, I have to take you even though I asked for a man." Seeing the stormy expression in her lovely blue-green eyes, he held up his hand. "Before you start screaming sex discrimination, let me explain. I wanted a male assistant because he could use the entire upstairs floor of my house and be available and ready whenever I got an emergency call. With a male assistant there wouldn't be any complications. No chance of a charge of sexual harassment—"

"Aaron, we know each other well enough to be sure there would never be a reason for a charge of sexual harassment. Please be honest with me and yourself. You're reluctant to hire me because of how we felt about each other all those months ago."

He looked at her silently for a long moment. "You're right. But don't you think it'll be awkward, us working together?"

"Maybe a little," she conceded, "but we're two professionals who should be able to work together."

"Anyway, it's a moot point. It looks like my request

has been overruled. I've got to take you, unless I want to get the department and the city involved in a law suit. With the present money shortage, that would be a dumb move, so I'm stuck with you."

The word "stuck" infuriated Karin. She had every intention of counting to ten before she spoke, but she made it only to three. "For your information, I didn't ask for this assignment. If you're stuck with me, then I'm just as stuck with you."

"Point taken," Aaron said gravely.

"Furthermore, I'm as good as, no, better, than any man you could have hired, and unless your memory's gone, you should know that too."

"Only my legs are gone."

Karin could feel the color drain from her face. "I didn't mean to imply . . . ," she faltered and broke off.

"I know you didn't." Aaron's voice was flat, his expression grim.

Karin watched him check his appointment book.

Finally he said, "Will you please sit down? I hate having to look up at people. That's one of the irritating results of being in this darn chair."

"Now you know how I always felt with you towering over me."

Aaron leaned back and looked straight at her. "At five foot ten in your stocking feet, you didn't have to look up far. If I remember correctly, and I'm sure I do, we were fairly well matched physically."

At a loss as to how to respond to that, Karin backed

up until her legs bumped the edge of the chair. She sat down. Aaron was right. When they'd held each other, their bodies had fit together perfectly. She quickly suppressed the bittersweet memory. It had no bearing on the present. It couldn't have. She had to swallow before she could speak.

"Is it me personally you object to, or the fact that I'm a woman?"

"I told you why I wanted a man for the job."

"Tell me again," she insisted.

"Because a male assistant could live in my upstairs rooms. That way if I got an emergency call, all I'd have to do is wheel myself to the bottom of the staircase and yell up at him. We could be on our way in five minutes. You know in a fire speed in responding is crucial."

"So, it's nothing personal."

"I didn't say that."

"No, you didn't. I've got to know. What do you hold against me personally?"

"You know darn well what. I asked you once to get out of my life and here you are again." Aaron saw her blanch and knew he'd hurt her once more. He hadn't meant to do that, but on the other hand, he hadn't expected or wanted her back in his life. She needed to know that, for both their sakes.

Karin didn't flinch or break eye contact. When she was sure her voice wouldn't quiver, she said, "I didn't even know you were back in Chicago, much less that you were the director of the new division. Don't worry. I won't ever throw myself at you again. Nor will I repeat that hospital scene. I don't make the same mistake twice, so you're perfectly safe. I'm here only in a professional capacity, and I'll leave the moment another position becomes open. In the meantime, I'd appreciate it if you treated me as you do any other arson investigator."

Aaron, who considered courage one of the more worthwhile human traits, couldn't repress a flash of admiration. She was some woman, the way she faced him, with a mixture of defiance, raw grit, and pride.

"Well?"

"That's fair enough," he said. Quickly, he turned his attention back to the photos on his desk.

Karin leaned back, her knees shaking. The burst of adrenaline was receding, leaving her weak and spent. Her hands trembled. She stuffed them under the folds of her full skirt to hide them. She was glad of the silence which enabled her to pull herself together.

"I was considering the guy who took these photos for my assistant, but you're right. He failed to take the single most important picture at the fire scene: the place where the fire started. You wouldn't have made that kind of mistake. How soon can you start?"

Karin opened her mouth and closed it again. Aaron's sudden reversal left her speechless. "Umm, how about tomorrow morning?"

"What? Waste an entire afternoon? Maybe that was okay in your former district, but it isn't in mine."

Karin was struck dumb by this outrageous allegation.

She had always worked long hours. When she started to protest, Aaron motioned for her to be quiet.

"I see that we're going to have to set a few ground rules," he said. "First, you're going to work harder than you've ever worked before. Can you take it?"

"Yes." Karin squared her shoulders.

"We'll see. Second, as my assistant you're on call twenty-four hours a day. When I call, you drop everything. Tell your boyfriend to get used to cold showers."

Before Karin could inform him that she didn't have the kind of boyfriend who'd need cold showers, Aaron continued.

"Can you handle that?" he demanded.

"Yes."

"Third, if you make a mistake, admit it and then rectify it. Okay?"

"Okay." Karin suppressed a shudder, remembering that Aaron's reprimands could strip the skin off a person's body. "Anything else?"

"Yeah. For the duration of our association, I own your time and your undivided attention. Understood?"

"Understood. How long do you think this will be?"

"Until I get out of this damn chair. Weeks, months. I don't know. What's the matter? Cold feet already?"

Aaron's voice had assumed a cutting edge. Was that because she had reminded him of his handicap? How sensitive was he about it? More important, how sure was he that he wouldn't have to stay in that chair for the rest of his life?

"Let's get one thing out in the open. I got hurt. Some of the doctors doubt that I'll ever get out of this wheelchair. They're wrong. But it will take time for my body to heal and get back to normal. In the meantime I can do most of the things I used to do. For those I can't, like sifting through the ashes at an arson site, I need you. You're going to be my legs and my spine. There's no use tiptoeing around my condition. You can refer to it. I'm not going to fall apart."

Karin nodded. "Thank you. That clarifies things." She stood and slung her bag over her shoulder. "What do you want me to do first?"

"Go over all our current cases and familiarize yourself with them. You'll find them in the library down the hall."

"Okay." Karin waited for a beat, but when he didn't say anything else, she shrugged and left.

Outside Aaron's office, Mrs. McKenzie stopped Karin. "Are you staying?" she asked.

"Looks like it."

"Good. I think you're the perfect choice even if *he*," she nodded towards Aaron's door, "doesn't realize it yet. Welcome aboard."

"Thanks." After Aaron's negative reaction, the friendly welcome was doubly appreciated. "I'm to start with the cases in the library.

"Follow me."

"Thank you, Mrs. McKenzie."

"Call me Molly. We're not formal around here. Yelling and slamming doors hardly goes with formality, does it?" Molly grinned engagingly.

"Is that the usual mode of communication?" Karin asked.

A dark look passed over Molly's face. "It didn't used to be like that so much, but since Aaron's accident—" Molly broke off. When they reached the library, she continued. "Aaron's injury is painful and most of the time he refuses to take the pain medication because it makes him groggy. When you're in pain, your temper's short. So, we make allowances."

"Have you worked for him for a long time?"

"Ten years. Ten good years despite this setback."

"Aaron said his injury isn't permanent. Is that true or wishful thinking?" Karin asked.

"The prognosis is fifty-fifty, but Aaron is determined to get out of that wheelchair and knowing his willpower and stubbornness, he undoubtedly will. Anyway, I'm rooting for him." Molly blinked rapidly to disperse the telltale tears that had gathered in her eyes. "Here are the arson cases we're currently investigating," she said, pointing to a long table.

Karin's heart sank when she saw the huge stacks of papers and photos.

"There's coffee next door and a couple of vending machines with snacks."

"Thanks, Molly."

"Well, good luck and remember the old saying about the bark being worse than the bite. It's true of our boss man."

Karin smiled weakly at Molly who left her with a friendly wave of her hand. The secretary obviously liked Aaron. Perhaps he wouldn't be such an ogre to work for.

Don't count on it though, she told herself. He had probably selected Molly from a large number of applicants while she had been forced upon him. The only thing that would mellow him toward her was hard work and results. With that in mind, Karin removed her jacket, rolled up the sleeves of her blouse, and reached for the nearest file. She read every piece of paper in it and summarized the contents on a yellow legal pad. Then she clipped the sheet to the front of the folder.

By 6:00 she'd made three trips to the coffee pot. Since she had been too nervous to eat anything all day, that much caffeine left her hands shaking. Though she was endowed with incredible stamina, she did need food. Eyeing the various machines, she saw that the only non-junk food item contained in any of them was a bar euphemistically billed as providing "health food and quick energy." The claims must have discouraged everybody else for the bar was quite hard and stale. Karin ate it only because the only alternative was an attack of low-blood sugar shakes.

A part of her hoped that Aaron would leave his office

to check on her and part of her was relieved that his door remained closed.

At 8:30 a tall man sauntered into the library. "Hi," he said. "You certainly are working late. My name is Don Knight. I'm Aaron's cousin."

Karin shook the hand he offered and introduced herself.

"So, where's the old slave driver? I've come to take him to physical therapy."

"I don't know," Karin said. "Have you looked in his office?"

"I'm right here," Aaron said, wheeling himself into the library.

"You should be ashamed of yourself. Making a love-ly lady work so late," Don scolded with a grin.

Aaron stared at his cousin coldly. "Miss Bergstrom will leave when she thinks she's done enough for the day. I don't make my people punch a time clock. Are you ready to go, Don?"

Of course, he didn't make them clock in their time, Karin reflected resentfully after the men left. Challenging their pride and their sense of achievement coerced Aaron's people not only to put in many more hours than they would otherwise, but work them volun-tarily and cheerfully. That was a psychologically clever move, but not so clever that she felt she had to stay beyond 9:00. By then she was weak with hunger, her head throbbed, and her shoulders were knotted with tension. Undoubtedly Aaron expected her to report back to work by nine, clear-eyed and eager. Slave driver wasn't an inappropriate description, she thought, reaching for her jacket.

Chapter Two

"How come you were in bed by the time I came home last night? It was only ten-thirty," Alice said, flopping down at the kitchen table. Stifling a prodigious yawn, she continued. "And how come you're already up and dressed, ready to go? It's not even seven o'clock yet."

"I was in bed that early because I worked till nine and was exhausted, and I'm up because my boss expects me back fresh and eager first thing this morning." Karin poured a cup of coffee and placed it before her sleepy roommate.

"The note you left on the 'fridge only said that you got the job as assistant to some head honcho in arson investigation. How was the first day on the job?"

"Don't ask."

51918

"That good, huh? Tell me about it." Alice sipped some coffee, waiting and watching Karin's face. After a lengthy silence, she asked, "It wasn't just the usual first-day hassle, was it?"

"No."

"What happened?"

"It's not what happened. It's who my new boss is."

"He's a real sleaze ball, huh? Well, you handled those Neanderthals at the fire station okay. He can't be much worse."

"My boss is Aaron Knight."

It took Alice a split second to make the connection. When she did, she set her cup down so hard, coffee sloshed over its rim. "Holy firecracker!" For a moment she was speechless. Then, mopping up the spill with a paper napkin, she asked, "How did he act when he saw you? What did he say?"

"Aaron didn't know I was coming, and to say that he was less than thrilled about having me shoved down his throat is the understatement of the century. Which means that I'll have to work twice as hard as anybody else and expect twice as many hassles."

"That's nothing new for you, is it?"

"No, but I keep hoping some day I'll get a job where that's not the case."

"Don't hold your breath waiting." Alice studied her roommate's face carefully. "Having to prove yourself isn't what's bugging you, is it?"

"No." Karin heaved a sigh. "I keep wondering if

accepting this job wasn't the biggest mistake of my life."

"Because you were once in love with him?"

"Yes."

"You're not still hung up on the guy?"

"Absolutely not."

"I should hope not. Not after the way he treated you in the hospital," Alice said, her eyes sparkling with righteous outrage.

"It's not only that," Karin murmured, thinking of their last argument and the reasons that had led up to it. Sighing, she added, "It's going to be awkward working with him. I don't know if I did the right thing taking this job."

Ever practical, Alice said, "You didn't really have any choice. It was either taking this job or standing in line at the unemployment office. I hear those lines down there are mighty long and the chance of getting a decent job are real slim."

"I know." Karin took a shuddering breath. "I guess time will tell whether I made the right decision."

"It was the *only* decision you could make. Remember that."

"I'll try. Anyway, I better get going." Karin rinsed her dishes and placed them in the dishwasher.

"When will you be home tonight?" Alice asked.

Karin lifted her shoulders in an elaborate shrug. "Who knows? Aaron expects us to work until we feel we've put in a good day's work."

"Oh brother. Give me a break." Alice rolled her eyes.

"I better get going. I want to be there at least half an hour early."

Before Karin left the apartment, she stopped to rub Vulcan's whiskers. The cat had shown up a couple of months ago, looking hungry and lost. Within a week's time, Vulcan had become the third tenant. He rewarded her with a loving flick of his pink tongue over the back of her hand.

Even though she arrived at 8:00, Aaron was already in the conference room, immaculately groomed, wearing gray slacks, a white shirt and a firmly knotted striped tie. Over the rim of his mug, he was watching her walk toward him. Karin hated being observed, especially when she had no clue to the observer's feelings. Maybe because she had recently petted Vulcan, Karin noticed that in daylight the man and the cat had eyes of the same unusual hue of yellow-gold. That was where the similarities ended, Karin thought. The cat was patient, gentle and affectionate—qualities she could not accuse Aaron of possessing.

"Have some coffee. Molly made it. It's good and strong," Aaron said in response to her greeting. "The blue mug is yours." When Karin looked at the mug wonderingly, he added in an offhand voice, "I had an extra one in my office."

That was a blatant lie, but Aaron didn't want Karin to know that he'd brought the mug from his home especially for her. He didn't want her to know that he'd been thinking about her. That he hadn't been able to stop thinking about her. His preoccupation with her last night had been due solely to her unexpected reappearance in his life, he told himself yet again. As soon as he got used to the idea, she would be just another arson investigator on his team.

"Thank you," Karin said with a pleased smile.

Her smile was like sunshine in winter. It warmed him all over. He felt the corners of his mouth lift. As soon as Aaron became aware of his smiling response, his manner became businesslike. "Have a seat. Unless there's an emergency, we start the day with a brief, informal meeting right here."

Karin sat down. Within minutes, three male investigators joined them. After introductions each man reported his progress. All were ex-policemen who'd specialized in arson investigations. Aaron and Karin were the only true "smokies" on the team. Aaron made a few notes on a clipboard before he sent two of them out on assignments. The third, Bryan Ewald, sat down next to Karin and immediately indulged in the sort of flirtatious small talk that would lead him to make a pass at her later. She responded in a reserved manner, hoping to discourage him, but he was either so thick skinned or so sure of his success that he ignored the cool signals she sent him.

"Bryan, I realize that your new coworker is an attractive woman, but if you can tear yourself away from her, I have a job for you," Aaron said, his voice clipped.

"Drive down to the Indiana Avenue arson site and recheck the basement."

Bryan's voice and expression turned serious. "What am I looking for?"

"Anything that shouldn't be there or looks suspicious."

"Okay, but that sounds like a two-person job. Any chance of Karin going with me? I could initiate her in our way of reporting data." Turning to Karin, he explained, "It's a little different from the way you smokies do it."

"No." Aaron uttered the word with the force of a high-velocity bullet. "Pick up Simon in the lab and take him."

"Well, in that case I'm off. Catch you guys later," he said good-naturedly and left.

An uneasy silence descended on the room until the sound of Bryan's footsteps grew faint.

"I would appreciate it if you didn't flirt with my men. It's bad for morale."

"Me? I wasn't flirting. Bryan was. Don't you dare put that on me!" Karin knew her voice had risen half an octave but she was so angry she couldn't lower her tone. She took two quick shallow breaths, trying to master her outrage. "You haven't changed, have you? If you had listened," she ground out, impaling Aaron with furious eyes, "You would have heard me try to discourage Bryan. It isn't my fault he's so dense or so vain that he couldn't perceive that."

Ruefully Aaron admitted to himself that Karin was

right. She hadn't flirted. Could it be that he was jealous? He loathed to think so, yet deep down he suspected that jealousy just might have motivated his reaction. He would have to watch himself. No way could he act that unprofessionally. And he could never let Karin guess his true feelings. He steeled himself. "Try harder. In my experience, all women can stop that kind of behavior in a man quickly if they want to."

"Don't you dare imply that I wanted him to flirt with me. Don't you dare!"

Karin bit her lower lip in an effort to gain control. Anger often caused tears to well up in her eyes. She hated that. Aaron was the last man on earth to whom she wanted to expose any of her vulnerabilities. With a supreme effort she prevented the tears from reaching her eyes.

"Yes, I could have stopped his flirting with a few words that would have cut him to the quick, but I don't like to be deliberately cruel. Besides, I have to work with him. Who knows, some day we may be at a fire scene together and my life may depend on him. It would be stupid to turn him into an enemy."

"You don't have to make him your enemy. Just behave professionally."

Karin drew herself up with icy dignity. "I always behave professionally, which is more than I can say for you or your men. If you want to improve manners around here, work on theirs and yours. That should keep you busy till Christmas. Now if you'll excuse me,

I have work to do in the library." Karin barely managed to keep herself from running from Aaron's office. As soon as she closed the library door behind her, she collapsed into the nearest chair, her knees weak, her hands trembling.

How dare Aaron blame her for Bryan's flirting? She didn't even find the man appealing, and even if she had, she would never behave like that on the job. Nor would she encourage a man to flirt with her in business circumstances. Why was it that women usually ended up being blamed for men's behavior toward them? It had started with Eve taking the rap for Adam, and things hadn't improved much since then. It was so unfair.

While she was still lamenting this deplorable fact, a new idea struck her. What if Aaron was trying to find or manufacture reasons for dismissing her? Would Aaron stoop so low? No, not unless he became convinced that she was bad for his department. Well, she wouldn't give him even the slightest reason to think so or the slightest excuse to fire her for any other reason. Nor would she let him panic her into quitting. She was there to stay until he regained the use of his legs or another position became available.

All she'd ever wanted was to become a firefighter like her father. All everyone she knew had ever done was pile obstacles into her path, starting with her mother and older sisters. They had never understood why she hadn't wanted to play dress-up, cuddle dolls or aspire to become a nurse or a movie star. If she played with dolls it was to rescue them from make-believe burning houses. If she dressed in costume, it invariably resembled a fireman's suit.

When her beloved father was killed in a fire, Karin had stoically endured the memorial service and the funeral, but had fallen apart during the reading of the will. He had left her his helmet, a gesture she recognized as his official approval for her to follow him into fire fighting. The helmet became her weapon against all her mother's objections, the strongest and most often cited of which were that the job was dangerous and that a woman reeking of smoke would never find a husband. What her mother was implying, of course, was that fire fighting was an unfeminine job.

Defined traditionally, it probably was, but any man who was so stuck in stereotypical roles didn't interest Karin. At twenty-five, she was in no hurry to get married. Sometimes she even thought she'd be better off remaining single. Unless, of course, a very special man came along. A man like Aaron.

Thinking of him, she recalled his unfair accusation. Aaron had overreacted. Almost as if he'd been jealous. Karin brought that wayward, wonderful thought to an abrupt stop. Now she was daydreaming. For some reason that probably had nothing to do with her, Aaron had been annoyed. That was all. Karin opened the top folder with a snap, forcing herself to concentrate on its contents.

Hours later, Molly stuck her head through the door. "Ready to go to lunch?"

Karin blinked, surprised. "I didn't realize it was so late. You're the first person who's opened the door all morning."

"All the men are out."

"Including Aaron?"

"No. He's holed up in his office." Molly wrinkled her forehead. "Funny. He didn't interrupt me even once all morning. That's a first. Wonder what's got into him." Then she shrugged, dismissing her boss's strangely quiet mood. "Are you ready to eat?"

"Yes, but I don't know if I can leave. Aaron was emphatic about my being available at all times."

"Oh pooh. You have a right to a lunch break. I'll tell him we're going."

Before Karin could restrain Molly, the secretary had left. When she came back, she carried her purse.

"We usually eat at the Cornucopia Cafeteria which is a block up the street. Is that okay with you?"

"Fine."

Ten minutes later they inched their way through the cafeteria's serving line.

"The food's okay, but bland," Molly said, shaking red pepper flakes liberally into her bowl of chili.

Over coffee, Karin tried to steer the conversation to Aaron without being obvious about it.

"Why don't you just ask me?" Molly suggested after Karin hemmed and hawed for while.

"Pardon?"

"What you want to know about the boss man."

"So much for trying to be subtle," Karin said, her face pink with embarrassment.

Molly grinned. "I'm sixty-three. I'm a grandmother seven times over. There isn't much about people I don't know or much that surprises me about them anymore. There are no women in his life at the moment, if that's what you were wondering about."

"I wasn't. I'm not interested in the personal side of his life." Karin realized she didn't sound very convincing. Nor was this strictly true. Quickly she added, "I'd like to succeed in this job. It's important to me, but, as you know, Aaron doesn't really want me as his assistant. I feel like I'm starting with three strikes against me."

"Just do the best job you possibly can. Ignore his temper. Stand up to him when you know you're right. Get enough rest and food so you can keep up with him and you'll be okay."

"You make it sound so easy."

"Easy? No. He's not an easy man to work with, but once he accepts you as a member of his team, he'll argue your case before Lucifer himself."

"What are my chances of him accepting me as a team member?"

"You want the truth?"

Karin nodded, steeling herself.

"Ordinarily, all a person would have to do is be professional and truly competent, but for some reason you're like a burr under his saddle. Do you have any idea why you have that affect on him?"

"He has probably never had anybody forced onto his team before," Karin said evasively. She didn't want to reveal their past relationship. She had been in love with Aaron. She wasn't certain how deeply he'd felt about her. They had been passionately attracted to each other, but he had never truly shared himself emotionally with her. Perhaps in time they could have reached the emotional intimacy she'd craved, but fate had intervened. A burning ceiling had ended their chance. Now he was her boss, and she was nothing more than an irritant in his existence.

After a thoughtful silence Molly said, "Once Aaron said a peculiar thing. It was when a woman he used to know telephoned several times and he asked me not to put her calls through any more. He mumbled something about being 'damaged goods' and not fit for a woman's love. Have you ever heard anything as ridiculous as that? My stars! If love were reserved only for the deserving, most of us would go without it."

Karin had heard a statement every bit as ridiculous in the hospital, only it had been phrased less gently. *Half a man,* he'd called himself, and when she had protested that the wheelchair didn't matter to her, he had called her a young, naïve fool and told her to get out of his life. The memory of that encounter still made her cringe.

"For all their claims of being logical and rational, men can glom onto the most unreasonable and ridiculous notions." Molly shook her head. With a sigh she asked, "Are you ready to go?"

They were silent on the way back to headquarters.

No sooner had Karin resumed her study of pending cases, when Aaron joined her in the library.

"Ready for some fieldwork?" he asked.

"Yes!"

"You don't sound like you're too crazy about paperwork either," he commented.

"It's necessary, but that's about all I can say about it. Where are we going?"

"To the building in the photos I showed you. I want you to rephotograph the scene."

"Okay." From his face, Karin could tell Aaron wanted to say something else to her. If she didn't know any better, she would have said he was at a loss for words.

"About before—" Aaron broke off, staring at the floor.

"Yes?"

"I was out of line about accusing you of flirting with Bryan. I guess I never realized it before, but he flirts with every woman he meets."

Karin was silent until it became obvious that this was all Aaron was going to say. "I accept your apology."

"About Bryan . . ."

"I never date the men I work with, so you don't have to worry about on-the-job entanglements."

"Good. I don't let anything interfere with the work.

Yours or mine or my men's," Aaron warned. "How soon can you be ready to go?"

"I'll have to go home to change, but I can be back in ninety minutes."

"Make it sixty."

"Sixty? Impossible. Seventy. Not a second less."

"And not a second more. We've got lots to do, and you don't have to look stylish to crawl through a burned building."

"I know that. But by the time I get to my car, drive home, change clothes, drive to—" Karin broke off, frowning. "By the way, where is the site?"

"Come back here to pick me up. We'll leave from here."

"I drive a compact car. Your chair won't fit into it."

"It won't have to if you can drive a van. I assume you do since it was one of my requirements that I doubt even Chief Edwards would ignore."

"I can drive a van."

Aaron glanced at his watch. "You've already used up a minute and a half."

"No, I haven't. The countdown doesn't start until I'm through that door." Karin hurried out.

"You love having the last word, don't you?" Aaron called after her.

From the reception room she yelled back, "Just like you." Karin winked at Molly who'd listened to the exchange with a grin.

If she got a speeding ticket it would be Aaron's fault,

Karin reflected, checking the rearview mirror again. There simply was no fast way to get to her far North Side apartment from Aaron's office.

Her apartment was quiet. Alice, who was working on a master's degree, was undoubtedly camped out in the library. Vulcan hopped out of his basket to rub himself around Karin's long legs a few times before he resumed his nap.

Even though she was in a hurry, Karin couldn't resist touching the silk shantung material of her beige suit lovingly before she hung it in the closet. No matter how long her assistantship lasted, this was probably the last time Aaron would see her dressed up. Most of the time, covered with the heavy, shapeless protective clothing her job demanded and reeking of smoke, she would look like a creature from some subterranean region. Karin didn't think she was a vain woman, but occasionally she yearned for a more attractive work uniform.

She exchanged her pretty lace underwear for the sturdy cotton type that could withstand the heavy laundering necessary to remove the acrid smells generated by a fire. Topping that with jeans and a blue cotton work shirt, she pulled on heavy lace-up boots. She tossed a change of clothing into a gym bag and was ready to leave. On her way out she glanced at her watch. It had taken her less than five minutes to change. Satisfied, she smiled.

Even though she rushed into the arson department two minutes before the deadline, Aaron was waiting, fidgeting in his wheelchair. His eyes flicked over her, head to toe and back to her hair which she had braided and fastened with a coated rubber band.

Sensing his unspoken question, she explained, "I tuck it securely under my helmet. I haven't forgotten your lectures on safety." Karin held up the brilliant fluorescent green helmet with *Bergstrom* emblazoned on the front.

"Good. I'd hate to see that mane ignited by a spark. Let's go."

They took the freight elevator to a small parking lot tucked ingeniously between the service areas of several adjoining buildings.

"Molly assigned you a parking space across the street so you won't have to hunt for one each day," Aaron said. He tossed her the keys to the dark blue van parked before them. "Familiarize yourself with the dashboard and then lower the platform for my wheelchair."

When she thought she had memorized the location of the primary function dials, she lowered the platform which allowed Aaron to wheel himself into the van and station himself right behind her.

"Where to?" she asked, fastening her seat belt.

"Take the Dan Ryan south," Aaron instructed, "and exit west on Garfield."

At that time of the afternoon the north-south expressway wasn't yet the nightmare of bumper-to-bumper traffic it would be during rush hour. Even so, stretches of it were being resurfaced, resulting in closed lanes and heavy traffic.

Not feeling that familiar with the idiosyncrasies of the van and being keenly aware of Aaron looking over her shoulder, Karin devoted all her concentration to her driving. When a small compact car cut right in front of her, she had to swerve sharply to avoid hitting it.

"You're doing fine," Aaron assured her.

Karin almost jumped out of the seat when he placed his hand on her shoulder.

"Relax," he said.

She realized he meant the gesture to be reassuring and calming, but to her it was anything but that. She felt as if some of his restless energy leaped into her, singeing her nerve ends, setting her molecules careening off each other, sending her pulse rate soaring. This couldn't be happening to her, she thought desperately, gripping the steering wheel till her knuckles turned white.

"The Garfield exit is coming up soon," Aaron informed her. He removed his hand from her shoulder to pick up a floor plan of the arson site.

Karin breathed easier. Her death grip on the wheel relaxed.

"Once we're on Garfield, it's only a couple of blocks."

Karin thought she'd felt his breath warm and intimate on her cheek when he'd spoken, but that couldn't be. She risked a look at him in the rearview mirror and froze. Unprepared for the penetrating gaze of his eyes, she was trapped by them for several beats before she could break free. Fortunately the van was still in its lane and not speeding off over the embankment.

This would never do, she sternly lectured herself. She was bound to find herself close to Aaron, meet his eyes, feel the casual or accidental touch of his hand during the course of their work day. She had to learn to react with equanimity and indifference. Or at least with seeming indifference. For the rest of the trip, Karin didn't take her eyes off the road once.

The burned building with its begrimed and blackened walls and broken windows fit right into the neighborhood, which looked like a recent combat zone. Many of the dilapidated houses were boarded up. The lots where buildings had been razed by fires or condemnation orders were littered with the hulks of abandoned cars, discarded furniture, bottles, cans and the debris of transient lives. Incongruously, half a dozen children played an energetic game of stick ball farther down the block.

When a car filled with curious and defiant-eyed teenaged boys passed them, blaring out loud rap music, Aaron handed Karin a walkie-talkie.

"Keep in touch with me at all times. I don't care if you merely recite 'Mary Had a Little Lamb'. I want to know where you are," he ordered.

Karin nodded, slipping the strap of the radio around

her neck. After she'd donned the helmet and the bright yellow-green duster that protected her from her neck to her safety shoes, she grabbed the tripod and thirty-five millimeter camera and proceeded towards the entrance of the burned building.

"Remember, stay in constant contact," he urged.

"I will."

Karin proceeded slowly, methodically, carefully setting up each shot and recording it in her notebook. This would be a textbook case, she vowed. She wasn't about to give Aaron a chance to criticize her work.

After a while she became so engrossed in her work that she forgot to check in with him. Aaron's loud voice erupting from the walkie-talkie caused her hand to jerk on the camera.

"Aaron, don't do that. You made me mess up a shot, not to mention what you did to my blood pressure."

"Then report in as you were told to do."

His displeasure was recognizable even over the static. "Sorry, I found something rather unusual and forgot," she apologized.

"The point of origin of the fire?"

"I'm not sure," she admitted. "I wish you could come in to see this."

"No more than I do," he said, his tone dry.

Karin flushed when she realized what she'd said. "I'm sorry."

Ignoring her apology, Aaron said, "Take several shots. Then let's get back to headquarters so you can develop the film and I'll take a look at what's puzzling you. Are you about done?"

"Yes. Let me finish this roll before the light goes completely." Karin heard him mutter to hurry up in that characteristic impatient tone. He had never been a model of forbearance, but his frustration at being confined to the wheelchair had robbed him of whatever patience he'd possessed. Knowing how hard it was for a dynamic man like Aaron to sit and wait, she worked as fast as she could, but still it took another half hour of concentrated effort before she rejoined him outside.

Karin removed the helmet which was both hot and heavy. Lifting her face toward the early evening breeze, she took a deep breath. Though the air here still smelled of smoke, it wasn't anywhere near as pungent as it had been in the building.

"Are you okay?" he asked, watching her.

"Sure. I just wish a fire site smelled a bit more like lilies of the valley," Karin said, wrinkling her nose. "Are there showers at headquarters?"

"Of course. Have you ever met an arson investigator who didn't want to strip and shower as soon as he left the site?"

"Is there going to be a problem with the shower? I mean with me being a *she* instead of a *he?*"

"Blast. I hadn't even thought of that." Aaron looked at her thoughtfully. "But don't worry. We'll improvise. Let's get going."

Chapter Three

Even though they caught the tail end of the evening rush hour, Karin felt more secure driving the van. After she'd pulled off the Dan Ryan, the streets on the near south side were relatively quiet. Stopped at a red traffic light, Karin heard an odd, low rumble. It sounded suspiciously like a hungry stomach. She glanced over her shoulder at Aaron. "When did you eat last?" she demanded.

"Don't you start in on me, too. It's enough Molly appointed herself my mother. I don't fancy you in that role."

Karin didn't fancy herself in that role either. "Shall I stop at a fast-food restaurant?"

"No. We'll send out for pizza. You may as well know we do that a lot to save time. What do you like on yours?"

43

"Mushrooms and green peppers."

"There's a refrigerator in the conference room. If you want to bring food from home, you can keep it in there."

"I don't know if you remember, but I don't usually eat meat, so I'll probably bring my meals." She watched his face in the mirror.

"I remember."

Under his breath, he added, "I remember everything."

Their glances met in the rearview mirror. For an instant they shared a mute acknowledgment of the attachment that had been between them, an attachment that had grown more intense from the first day they'd met. Quickly, Karin lowered her eyes to the road before them. Thoughts of their past were dangerous. Dangerous and counterproductive. They were both silent for the rest of the drive.

Back at headquarters, Karin placed her helmet and protective clothing into the trunk of her car before she took the stairs to Aaron's office on the second floor.

"The shower room is ready for you," Aaron told her. "Follow me."

Farther down the hall he opened a walk-in closet containing cleaning supplies, rolled his chair through to the door in its back wall and pounded on it. "Anyone in there?" When no one answered, he opened the door. "Wait here, just in case." Then he grinned at her. "Unless you don't mind meeting some of your male colleagues in the altogether?"

Karin hastily stepped back. "No, no. You go and look."

He returned moments later. "The showers are all yours. Just don't open the door at the other end."

"Why not? What's in there?"

"The men's room."

"Oh. What's to keep someone from entering the shower room from there?"

"Because someone will be stationed there to prevent that."

"Who?"

"Me. In a few days you'll have your own bathroom. The work order to put partitions in has been approved."

"Thank you."

"You have ten minutes."

"Ten?"

"That's all. Take longer and I'll come in to get you."

Thinking she'd heard a suggestive note in his voice, Karin's eyes flew to Aaron's face. He was grinning at her. For a moment he was the man she'd known and fallen in love with. In wonder Karin held her breath. Time seemed suspended. Then she saw the teasing light fade from his hazel eyes, and she knew he had remembered his injured legs. Without a word, he whipped the chair around and wheeled himself away.

Karin hurried into the nearest shower cubicle. Pounding her fists against its ceramic tile wall, she muttered several unkind words. How could she let herself get sucked into the past, into remembering what it had been like between them? That way lay madness. Aaron had made it brutally plain that day in the hospital that what had been building between them was over.

Was she to blame for his accident? At least in part? Had she upset him so with their argument that he'd been distracted, careless? Hysterically she'd accused herself of that at his beside, and he hadn't denied it. Of course, he'd been nearly out of his mind from the physical pain of his injuries. That wrenching scene between them hadn't helped. The nurse had ordered Karin to leave as she jabbed a needle into Aaron's arm.

Karin hadn't seen Aaron again until she'd walked into the office of the South Side Arson Investigation Division. Unclenching her fists, she vowed to deal with the present only. Heaven knew that was quite a job in itself, given the number of arson cases that waited to be investigated. Work, that was what her life at the moment was all about. Nothing else.

Resolutely, she pulled back the curtain and turned on the water. She undressed quickly. Moments later she stepped under the hot spray with a sigh of relief.

She would have enjoyed spending her allotted time just standing under the water, but that was impossible. To remove the fire stench that clung tenaciously to skin and hair, she needed to scrub every inch of her body with a specially designed shampoo and soap. Aware of every fleeting second, she hurried through the routine. Her body was still damp when she pulled on clean underwear, jeans and a tee shirt. She ran a comb through her wet hair, wondering if she dared take the time to dry it. In the end, the professional in her decided it was better to be punctual than look pretty, even though the woman in her protested that decision.

Karin entered the conference room feeling like a drowned mouse.

"You're still punctual. I like that."

Aaron's small praise pleased her out of all proportion; just as it had always done in the past, she reflected morosely. She was prepared to bet her last dollar that every female student he'd ever taught had felt the same way. When he chose, Aaron could be lethally charming. And he possessed a charisma that drew women like flowers lured bees.

"Sit down." Aaron pointed to the chair next to him. "You may as well read these reports while we wait for the food. They will familiarize you with the work your colleagues are currently doing. No sense in wasting time."

Karin sat next to him and reached for the folder.

"Is that lilies of the valley?" he asked.

When she looked at him bewildered, he explained.

"Your perfume. Earlier you said that you like the smell of lilies of the valley."

"My perfume? Oh." Aaron must be referring to the lotion she had smoothed over her skin to counteract the strong soap. "I hadn't realized the scent of my moisturizing lotion was that noticeable. It's a floral bouquet with lilies of the valley," she said, not wanting Aaron to think she wore perfume. At the station house where she'd serve her probationary time, one of the unspoken and unwritten rules had been to do nothing to attract attention to yourself as a woman. That had precluded wearing makeup, cologne and jewelry.

Aaron leaned closer, his straight nose lifting like Vulcan sniffing an interesting aroma. "Remember how I tried to drum the importance of a trained sense of smell into you students at the academy? It's vital to arson investigations." To demonstrate, he inhaled her scent deeply, audibly. "I could find you in the dark," he murmured, "even without you wearing the lotion."

Karin's breath became shallow and rapid, knowing that Aaron's face was so close to hers that if she turned even a little, their lips would touch. She sat as if she'd been turned into a pillar of salt. "I remember," she said at last, keeping her eyes trained on the far wall. "We had to blindfold ourselves and then sniff a number of containers. I haven't felt the same about household ammonia since."

Aaron chuckled.

She sensed him drawing back. Only then did she dare glance in his direction out of the corner of her eyes. He was calmly reaching for a sheaf of papers. Following his example, Karin picked up the first page of the report and pretended to read it.

Her heart was beating fast. Too fast. This would never do, she thought in near panic. She couldn't keep reacting like this every time he came near her, but how could she prevent that? She risked another look at him. Aaron's head was bent over the papers. The overhead light brought out the auburn tones in his thick hair, making it gleam like rich, polished mahogany. Karin experienced the insane desire to stroke his hair the way she stroked Vulcan.

She tightened her hands around the report to prevent herself from succumbing to this dangerous impulse. Not only dangerous, but completely inappropriate. He'd made it clear in the hospital that the accident had ended his interest in her. Aaron seemed oblivious of her, totally absorbed in his reading. A spasm of resentment flicked through her. If he could be that indifferent, surely she could be, too. Perhaps if she concentrated on her work the way he did, she might become unaware of him. Even as she resolved to do that, she knew deep down that she could never manage that completely, but at least she had to try.

When the pizza was delivered fifteen minutes later, she noticed, pleased, that she had actually been caught up in the report.

"Put that away while we eat," he ordered, nodding toward the papers. "We don't want to get the reports greasy."

"I didn't think you wanted me to put them away so that we could have a civilized conversation while we ate."

Aaron shot her a long, level look. Then the corners of his firm, generously designed mouth turned up. "You never were intimidated by me, were you? Not even as a student. Always an irreverent attitude toward authority, right?"

"Right. Can't have those authority figures getting too big-headed," she quipped. He would never know that part of what he called an irreverent attitude had been a defense mechanism she used to protect herself against liking him too much. "It never upset you. My attitude, I mean."

"No. Let's go to the lunch room so we can get something to drink from the 'fridge," he suggested.

Carrying the pizza, Karin followed him. She opened the large refrigerator to look for something to drink.

"You want to know how I really feel about your irreverent attitude?" Aaron asked, setting out paper plates and napkins on the small, round table.

"Not really, but you're going to tell me anyway." Karin braced herself for his no doubt unflattering disclosure.

"I rather enjoyed our sparring. It's boring when students accept everything I say as gospel and feed it back to me on tests. You never did that. You challenged me at every turn."

"A lot of good it did me. You still made me do all those extra exercises," she flung at him.

Aaron grinned at her. "My way of protecting you. I wanted you to be up to anything you'd encounter at a fire. I made you tough enough to survive."

"Well, don't claim all the credit for that. I was the

one doing all those blasted push-ups and chin-ups," she said, her tone dry.

"Didn't hurt you, did it? You look exceptionally fit and strong." Aaron's eyes assessed her thoroughly, leisurely, as if to confirm his statement.

"Oh sure. Not a speck of makeup on and my hair wet," she said, self-consciously fingering a dank strand.

"You're not as elegant as you were this morning, but now you look like a competent, hard-working arson investigator," he said, his voice filled with satisfaction.

Being complimented by Aaron on her professional abilities meant a great deal to Karin. To hide her pleasure at his unexpected compliment, she turned back to the open refrigerator. "What would you like to drink?"

"Hand me three of those small cartons of milk."

Karin took cartons for each of them and returned to the table. "The pizza smells delicious," she said. Following his example, she served herself and started eating.

As they were eating, Aaron asked, "How's your mother? I didn't see her at the last ladies' auxiliary garden fest I had to attend."

Karin almost choked on the piece of pizza in her mouth. When she recovered, she asked, "How on earth do you know she is a member of the auxiliary?"

"I saw the name Bergstrom listed on the officers' roster, so I made it a point to look for her."

"You saw her only that one time at my apartment

when you were waiting for me. How could you have possibly recognized her?"

"That's easy. Her resemblance to you is startling. She's still a good-looking woman."

"Yes, she is, and she's fine." Belatedly, Karin realized that in a roundabout way Aaron had paid her a compliment.

"I seem to remember her telling me about being involved in a business of some kind. Flowers, was it?"

"She and my aunt run a floral shop in Schaumburg. Good grief. Did she confide our entire family history to you?"

"No. Mostly we talked about you. Your career and how quickly you'd made arson investigator."

"That must have been some conversation," Karin said, her voice dry. "My mother all but tied me up to keep me out of the fire department."

"She told me. But now she's proud of you." Noticing Karin's skeptical look, he said, "Surely she's told you that."

Karin shrugged. "My mother never compliments anyone directly, especially not her daughters. It might go to our heads."

"Are your sisters married?"

"Yes. Between them they've provided my mother with five grandchildren, which takes the pressure off me somewhat."

Aaron grinned at her. He finished the last piece of pizza. Then, as if he remembered that this was not a social occasion, or that Karin had prompted him into making small talk, he became all business again.

"Did you notice anything resembling a pattern as you read the reports of our last cases?"

Karin thought for a moment. "Pattern is perhaps too strong a word, but the location of that last arson fire was only one block from the site we covered today. And, of course, both structures were low-rent, residential hotels. It's too early to tell, but I think in both the same accelerant was used. And the fires started in similar locations. Only in the one we looked at today . . . I'll let you know my suspicion as soon as I develop and print the photos." Karin wiped her hands on the napkin and stood up. She reached for her camera and the rolls of film. "I saw the darkroom on the way in. I'll let you know as soon as the first photos are dry. Will you still be here?"

"Of course."

Of course. Sitting companionably with him, eating pizza, she had momentarily forgotten how totally dedicated to his job he'd always been, and how his single-mindedness had made her feel unneeded. Well, that was in the past, she reflected, hurrying to the photo lab.

The darkroom was well equipped. She worked quickly and efficiently. When she was finished, she carried the pictures to the conference room and tacked them up on the cork board. Aaron must have been listening for her because he joined her promptly.

Facing the cork board, she explained, "As you can

see, I started with the outside shots and continued as I entered the building by the side door. They're all fairly routine until I got to this storage area." Karin pointed to the photo.

Aaron studied it carefully. "Looks like the fire started here in the east wing. That's where the other investigator stopped taking photos. You didn't. Why?"

"Because if the fire started here, as it obviously did, it doesn't explain its spread. That's why I thought, and I think you agreed with me, that something was missing."

Aaron nodded, his eyes flicking to the remaining row of photos. "Go on."

"These are the shots of the lobby and these are the photos of the interior of the far west wing. If the fire started only in the east wing, how could there be so much damage way over here?" Karin tacked up the photo she'd been holding. "When I got to the west wing, I found this storage area which is almost a duplicate for the one in the east wing and, *voila*, we have another point of origin."

"The arsonist started two fires. I suspected as much. Good work, Karin."

"Thank you." Karin flushed with pleasure at his praise.

"I think he set the fire in the east wing first. Do you agree?" Aaron asked after a while.

"Yes. But I don't think much time elapsed between their start."

"No. He couldn't afford to have one fire discovered before the other was well under way also."

"But why start it in two places? What was the urgency?"

Aaron shook his head. "I don't know. Unless the arsonist tells us that when we catch him, we might never know."

"And the chances of catching him aren't that good, are they?"

"Statistically, no, but I have a hunch that we'll catch this one. His setting two fires in the same building strikes me as his being cocky. Sooner or later that quality will cause him to become careless."

"Do we have any good leads?"

"Not yet, but the investigation is just beginning." Aaron stared at the photos, but Karin had the feeling he was thinking of something else, that he was trying to make up his mind. When he did, he spoke.

"First thing in the morning we're going back to this other site. The Greyfox Manor. I have a hunch we . . . that is, you, will find something the other photographer overlooked."

"Like where a second fire was started?" Karin asked.

"That's what I want you to look for. I know three weeks have elapsed and the crime scene has been contaminated, but we can't afford to overlook anything."

"Okay, but there's no reason why you have to come along. It'll be a slow, painstaking process," Karin warned.

"Meaning?"

Aaron looked at her coldly through narrowed eyes. She swallowed, knowing he wasn't going to like what she was about to say. "Meaning that you'll be asking me every few minutes if I'm done."

"For your information, Karin Bergstrom, I've spent endless, countless hours sifting through debris looking for clues when you were still in high school."

"I know that, but that was before. . . . That was when you were able to look for clues yourself, not when you had to wait for someone else to do it for you," Karin said, bracing herself for the dismissal she was certain would follow her bold words. Well, she had always wondered what it was like flipping burgers for a living. Now she would have a chance to find out. The tension-filled silence stretched between them. Suddenly, she saw his broad shoulders relax.

"You're right. That's exactly what I would do and it would make you nervous and interfere with your efficiency. However, I can't leave you alone at the site. That area of Chicago isn't exactly safe. I'll take some of my endless paperwork along to keep busy while you investigate."

"If I were a man you wouldn't feel compelled to stay with me," Karin challenged.

"But you aren't a man, are you?"

"I can take care of myself. I won't have you babysit me. That's demeaning," Karin protested angrily.

Aaron took her hand, encircling her slender wrist.

"Listen to me, Karin. If you'd bothered to study the roster, you'd have seen that we always team up. Nobody investigates alone. That way if one team member is hurt, the other can go for help. It's only common sense to work that way."

"But—" Karin interjected.

Aaron placed the thumb of his other hand lightly over her lips. "*Sh*. Listen to me. Even if working with a partner wasn't policy in this department, if I said you weren't going alone, that order would stand. I'm the boss here. You can fight me on every issue you want, but on this one, you won't win."

Aaron's thumb lingered lightly on her lips. He'd forgotten how soft her mouth was, how lush her lower lip, how beautifully curved the upper, how eminently kissable. When Aaron realized where his thoughts were leading, he jerked his thumb away swiftly.

She missed his touch the moment he ended it. She had almost managed to forget how much she'd liked holding his hand, leaning her head against his shoulder when watching a movie, or simply gazing into his eyes. Quickly, she dismissed these bittersweet memories.

"When you were hurt, did you have a partner with you?" Karin asked. She caught her breath, appalled at having blurted out the question so starkly, a question she didn't think he would ever answer. When he did, his voice was carefully modulated, controlled, revealing to her that he was far from having come to terms with his near fatal accident.

"My partner got help for me within minutes. That's the only reason I'm not paralyzed for life. Or dead."

The fight went out of Karin. She couldn't argue with the logic of that statement. Inclining her head, she said quietly, "Okay, partner."

Aaron looked at Karin, wondering if she fully understood the seriousness, the necessity of working in pairs. Fire-damaged, abandoned structures drew derelicts, gangs, drug dealers, desperate loners and heaven only knew who else. The thought of her alone in such a place caused his scalp to tighten with apprehension. Gently he tugged at her wrist, forcing her to look at him directly.

"Karin, I mean it about not investigating on your own. Don't do it."

"I know you do, and I understand. Truly."

Reassured by what he saw in her lovely eyes, he said, "Why don't you write up a brief report to go with those photos and then call it a day. Bring it to my office before you leave."

"All right." Aaron shifted his gaze back to the photos. After several seconds, Karin wondered if he'd forgotten that his hand still encircled her wrist. She certainly had not. His fingers were warm and strong, exerting just enough soft pressure to make her cognizant of his touch but gentle enough not to hurt. Even if his touch had been as light as a butterfly's, she would have been achingly aware of it. He was still studying the displayed pictures. She must have moved. Aaron obviously noticed he was still holding her hand. He dropped it as if it had suddenly turned into a red-hot poker. Without looking at her, he wheeled himself toward the door.

"Don's taking me to therapy in half an hour. I want to see your report before I leave," he said over his shoulder.

When Aaron was gone, Karin rubbed the wrist he'd held. The skin tingled as if his touch had been a brand. She was being fanciful again, she told herself. Branding her had been the farthest thing from Aaron's mind and if she wanted to get the report written in time, they had best be light years from hers as well.

Within ten minutes, she entered Aaron's office to hand him the one-page report. While he was reading it, the phone rang. Since Molly had left hours earlier, he answered it.

"It's for you."

Surprise and alarm shot through Karin. Her family never called her at work unless it was an emergency. She picked up the receiver with a shaking hand.

"Have you forgotten you have a date?" Alice demanded without preamble.

"Oh no! I did. It completely slipped my mind. Is Jason there?"

"Yes. He's been waiting for almost an hour. I'll put him on."

"No, don't. Just tell Jason—" But her plea came too

late. Seconds later, Jason wanted to know where she was. "I'm still at work. I'm sorry, but there's no way I can make it to the north side in time for the late showing." Karin listened to Jason's politely-phrased complaints and reminders that this was the last night the movie was being shown, all the time uncomfortably aware of Aaron's presence. He didn't even pretend not to listen.

"Look, I'm sorry. I didn't mean to stand you up. Honestly, I didn't. Something came up at work." She paused to take a breath. Then she had a brilliant thought. "I have an idea. Why don't you take Alice? She loves science fiction and special effects as much as you do." Karin glanced at her watch. "If you hurry, you can still make it. I'd really feel awful if you miss this movie because I was detained. Ask Alice. I'm sure she'd like to go." Karin waited while a hurried consultation took place at the other end. A few seconds later she said, visibly relieved, "I told you she'd like to go. Enjoy the film." Handing the receiver back to Aaron, she met his amused glance.

"Detained at work?"

The irony in his voice made her feel defensive. "Okay, so I plain forgot, but I thought if I told him that on top of standing him up, I'd really hurt his feelings."

"I don't know about Jason, but I always prefer the truth."

Feeling the need to justify herself, Karin said, "I

think little white lies are acceptable occasionally, especially when they avoid inflicting unnecessary pain."

"Sometimes pain is the only thing that assures you that you're still alive."

Surprised by this brooding aside, Karin studied Aaron's face which looked suddenly pale and drawn. Before she could ask if he felt all right, he spoke.

"Does Jason usually let himself be fobbed off on your roommate?"

"I didn't fob him off," Karin said, stung. "He really wanted to see this movie. I saw no reason why he should have to go alone when Alice would like to see it, too."

"I sure wouldn't allow you to pass me on like a cast off pair of pants."

"I didn't do that!" Karin glowered at Aaron. Her frown didn't seem to faze him for he had a pleased, Cheshire catlike expression on his face.

"It's just as well that you're not that serious about Jason."

"I didn't say I wasn't serious about him. We've been friends for years, and I take our friendship seriously."

"Friends?" Aaron's voice dripped with disbelief.

"Yes, friends. We act as each other's escorts when we attend functions where we absolutely must have an escort, and we do fun things because we enjoy each other's company." Seeing his frankly skeptical expression, Karin said, "Why do you find that so hard to believe?"

"In my experience, men and women can be coworkers, colleagues, acquaintances, lovers, husbands and wives, but not friends."

Karin shot him a long, observing look. He really seemed to believe that. She was about to make some scathing remark when it occurred to her to wonder if she could be friends with Aaron. No, never! Not when his most casual touch heated her skin and caused her pulse to leap crazily. More subdued, she added, "Perhaps friendship is possible only between certain men and women."

Aaron's raised eyebrow expressed his skepticism. "As I was saying, it's good you're . . . only 'friends' with him, because you know firefighters are on call twenty-four hours at a time. That could ruin a romance fast. Is he the only—"

"You said I could leave as soon as I finished the report. I finished it," she snapped.

"So you did."

Karin saw him shift in his wheelchair, saw the white look around his mouth and knew Aaron was in considerable pain. Instantly, she was sorry she had snapped at his probing. "Can I help you? Can I get you anything? A glass of water? A pain pill?"

"No! I can manage," he ground out. A fine sheen of perspiration beaded his forehead. His eyes glittered fiercely when he dismissed her. "That'll be all. Get out of here, Bergstrom. I don't need you."

His terse, surly rejection hit her like an undeserved

slap across the face. Without a word, Karin turned and fled from the room, fighting the hurt that tore at her soul.

All the way home she berated herself bitterly. She knew better than to offer Aaron anything, especially her help. He hadn't needed her help in the past and he didn't want it now. All he wanted from her was hard work. In the future that's all he would get from her.

"May my tongue wither and fall out if I ever offer him help or sympathy again," she vowed, hardening her soft, wounded heart.

Chapter Four

The telephone must have rung twice before the sound penetrated her first deep sleep of the night. When it did, Karin's body jerked into a sitting position. One hand reached to switch on the bedside lamp while the other snatched up the receiver.

"Karin Bergstrom speaking."

"There's another fire. Pick me up. Do you have my address?"

"Yes. No. I mean, I remember the address of your apartment, but I don't know where you live now."

He told her how to get to his house. "You'll have to drive to the office to get to the van and then pick me up."

"Okay. Where's the fire?" she asked, but Aaron had already hung up. It had to be near the other arson sites where they were trying to establish a pattern or he wouldn't have called her in the middle of the night.

Correction. It was only 2:15, hardly the middle of the night, not when she hadn't gone to bed until 11:30. She had worked until 9:00 every evening for the past two weeks. By the time she got home, laundered her smoke-soaked work clothes and did a few chores, it was after 11:00. Her apartment was just too far away, she reflected again, as she quickly slipped into the clothes she'd laid out before going to bed. She sluiced her face with cold water, brushed her teeth, and was out the door in record time.

Stopped at a traffic light in the three-block area near her apartment which was heavily populated with a variety of night spots, Karin watched the Friday night crowd. Couples leaving the bars had their arms wrapped around each other, oblivious of everyone else. With a catch in her throat, she remembered the last night when she and Aaron had been just like that. They had listened to a band playing in the cellar below their favorite bar, which was unexpectedly good. The quintet's style was unmistakably rooted in the Mississippi blues that characterized the early Chicago music scene.

At the start of the group's second set, Aaron had drawn her onto the handkerchief-sized dance floor where the crowd left them no choice but to hold each other so close not even a wisp of smoke could have insinuated itself between their bodies. Karin closed her eyes, remembering the sound and the smell of the place. Most of all though, she remembered Aaron's touch: his lean jaw resting against her temple, his breath warm on her hair, one hand enfolding hers, the other laid lightly against the small of her back to guide her around the dance floor. At times they had looked into each other's eyes for long minutes, silently acknowledging the powerful attraction between them.

That had been the night almost two years ago when that burning ceiling collapsed on Aaron, putting him into a wheelchair and her out of his life.

He didn't have to go to that fire. He hadn't been on call. Yet when he received the beeper message, he'd chosen his job over her yet one more time. They'd argued fiercely. She had accused him of not wanting or needing her, of not caring as deeply about her as she cared about him. He'd protested that he did, but when all was said and done, he'd elected to go. An hour later that ceiling had collapsed, ending everything.

The loud horn blast from an impatient driver behind her jolted Karin from her painful memories. Just as well, she thought, as she stepped on the gas and shot through the intersection.

When she arrived at Aaron's house with the van, he was already sitting at the bottom of the drive, impatience written all over him. At first she had wondered why he hadn't asked for hand controls so he could drive the van himself. Then she had realized that such a request would be an admission that his recovery would take a long time, or worse, that he would never walk again. A man like Aaron confined to a wheelchair for the rest of his life . . . Karin shuddered, unable to consider what that would do to him.

Quickly, she lowered the platform for him.

"You took long enough," Aaron grumbled, looking at his watch.

"I drove a good twenty miles above the speed limit. It's a wonder I didn't get pulled over by a patrol car."

"We're going to have to do something about your living arrangements."

Karin turned her head to look at him.

"But not now. Head south. Take the Garfield exit."

"So the fire *is* in the same area. This definitely establishes a pattern." Excitement bubbled through Karin. Perhaps they were getting closer to finding answers to the rash of arsons that had plagued this area during the last month.

Aaron didn't say anything, but she could tell by his posture, by his eyes, that he, too, shared her excitement. He wore a yellow, short-sleeved shirt, a tie, and a pair of cotton slacks. Despite the humid August night, the creases in his slacks were sharp, his shirt crisp and unwrinkled. He always looked good, she thought. She allowed herself the pleasure of gazing at him a moment longer before she switched off the overhead light and started the motor.

They were still several blocks from the fire when they heard the sirens of additional fire trucks and patrol cars hurrying to the blaze.

"Sounds like a big one." He swore under his breath.

Karin perceived the frustration in Aaron's voice. "Maybe this one's due to natural causes."

"Don't count on it."

Heavy, black smoke was pouring through the first floor windows of the furniture store. "At least they didn't have to go looking for the fire," Karin said, more to herself, knowing how she had hated entering a building without knowing exactly where the fire was located. That was like venturing into a dense stand of trees where a dangerous animal lurked.

"Let's go," Aaron said. "I feel like an old fire horse. One whiff of smoke and I'm rearing to go."

Karin pinned her ID to her shirt, scooped her helmet onto her head and grabbed the camera and tripod. Aaron was already at the perimeter, studying the scene.

"Did you notice the color of the smoke?" he asked.

"Uh-huh. Black," she murmured, setting up the tripod.

"What do you bet it's arson, and that a hydrocarbon accelerant was used to set it?"

"No bet. Unless chemicals were stored on the premises. You know, for touch-up repairs and refinishing," Karin said, setting the shutter speed and f-stop as low as she could to capture the night scene.

"This is strictly a retail furniture store. I doubt that

they'd have significant amounts of chemicals in the place."

Aaron rubbed his chin which was covered with the beginnings of a beard. It probably wouldn't take him long to grow one, Karin thought, glancing at him between takes. He would look good with a close-cropped, dark beard. Like an adventurer or an explorer.

"It's spreading too fast for it not to be arson. The sprinklers probably aren't working," he said.

Karin murmured agreement and quickly bent over the camera. She had to stop daydreaming on the job. Inattention would lead her to make mistakes. Aaron would be displeased and that's the one thing she wanted to avoid. Oh rats, Karin thought, she was doing it again. Trying to win his praise. *Just do your job,* she told herself grimly. When she'd taken half a roll of film of the burning building, she removed the camera from the tripod.

"Do you want me to walk around and get some candid shots of our spectators?" she asked Aaron, wiping the sweat from her forehead. The combined heat of the fire and the muggy night was intense.

"I doubt that this fire was set by a pyromaniac."

"Since all the other fires in the area were the work of a professional torch, I think you're probably right."

"But to be on the safe side, do it. Just don't wander off." Aaron raised his hand to stop her objection when he saw her expression. "And, yes, I'd say this to you if you were a man. I need you to help me interview the men as soon as they finish their primary search."

"Okay." Karin walked around, keeping to the shadows, studying the face and the body language of the people staring at the burning building. She saw and sensed nothing but the usual interest displayed by spectators. After making a slow circle, she rejoined Aaron.

They interviewed the fire fighters as they staggered out of the building, grimy, sweaty, and exhausted. The lieutenant in charge of the first on-site fire truck told them that a passing motorist reported the fire. In his opinion, based on fifteen years of experience, this was a deliberately set fire. He, too, had noticed the black, thick smoke that suggested a chemical accelerant. He also informed them that the back door had been jimmied and that the sprinkler system didn't work, just as Aaron had suspected.

Aaron supervised the perimeter being cordoned off to secure the fire scene from contamination. They made one last circuit around the site after everyone left. Only then did Aaron turn his wheelchair in the direction of the van.

"Well, since we can't do anything else around here until the place has cooled down, we may as well grab a few hours of sleep," he suggested.

That made sense to Karin. She knew she was in for a busy, tiring day. If only she didn't have to waste precious time commuting back to her apartment. Then an idea struck her. Why couldn't she curl up in the back of the van? If she locked the doors she should be safe in Aaron's parking space behind his house. Before she could mention this, he spoke.

"It'll be too time consuming to drive all the way to the office to pick up your car and then to your North Side apartment."

"I know. I'll curl up in the back of the van to sleep."

"Over my dead body! Have you lost your mind?"

"I'll lock the doors. Your neighborhood seems safe enough," Karin said defensively.

"No neighborhood is safe enough for that. You'll sleep in my house."

The ring of absolute authority in Aaron's voice told Karin that her protests would be in vain, but still she felt compelled to say, "I can't impose on you like that."

Aaron's eyes narrowed as he looked at her. "What's the real reason you don't want to sleep in my house, Bergstrom? Afraid to tarnish your reputation?"

"No, of course not," she protested hotly. "I'm not so thin-skinned. Nor am I particularly worried about what people say or think. Besides, you're the most disciplined man I ever met." She pivoted and walked rapidly away from him.

Watching her stalk long-legged toward the van, Aaron wasn't so sure about his discipline. He'd always loved to watch her walk: graceful and purposeful, like a warrior princess out of a Nordic fairy tale. Since he'd started physical therapy he'd become preoccupied, if not obsessed, with muscles, sinews and tendons. He noted that Karin appeared to be in top condition still. He liked that. He'd always admired bodies that were disciplined and honed to perfection. Glancing down at his near-useless legs, he grimaced in pain and distaste. Once again he swore that he'd sooner die than live with a half-dead body.

Pressing his lips into a resolute line, he propelled himself toward the van and the tired woman standing beside it. Karin had lowered the platform for him. Without a word he rolled himself inside.

Neither spoke on the drive to his house. Karin parked the van in his parking space off the alley. She sat as if undecided what she planned to do. Aaron reached forward to the dash to lower the platform.

"Are you coming?" he asked.

Karin got out. She had no choice, not unless she was ready to let Aaron Knight know that spending the night under his roof bothered her. If it didn't bother him, she'd submit to torture before she'd admit that the thought of sleeping in his house made her heart beat loudly and caused her lungs to draw in air raggedly. She was so tired that she ought to fall asleep immediately. That was, if she could get her mind off Aaron. Fat chance, she thought glumly. She had trouble doing that when she was miles away from him. Heaven only knew what it was going to be like sleeping only one floor above him.

Karin took a deep breath. Ready or not, she couldn't delay any longer. She followed him through the small fenced back yard, up the ramp to the back porch and into the house through the utility room.

"Let me explain the layout to you." Aaron wheeled his chair slowly down the wide hallway running from the front to the back, dividing the house in half. "On my left is the kitchen. Next to it is the dining room which I now use as my bedroom. The living room is at the front of the house and a bathroom is tucked under the staircase."

Karin looked into each room they passed. "Your house is beautiful," she exclaimed. "I love it. All this wood. And the high ceilings and the unusual windows. I know this isn't Victorian, but what is this style called?"

Aaron's mouth quirked into a small smile at her enthusiasm. "I'm not sure the style has a name. The only thing I've heard the house referred to is as an example of the American Arts and Crafts movement."

Karin returned to the living room for another look. Centered on the long outside wall was a large fieldstone fireplace flanked by built-in bookcases reaching half-way up the wall. Both the glass doors of the bookcases and the small windows above them were adorned with an unusual grid design. Passing his bedroom, she noticed that he slept on a metal hospital bed. It was probably the only kind he could get in and out of of alone. Seeing him watch her, she asked, "Have you lived here long?"

"Several months. My fifth-floor apartment wasn't

set up for a wheelchair. I bought this house partially furnished."

As if he regretted that slip of personal information, Aaron's brows drew together in a frown. "Sorry. You must be dead on your feet and I'm going on about the house like a real estate agent."

"It's okay. I asked because I'm interested."

"My cousin Don sometimes spends the night, but this being Friday, my part-time housekeeper changed the bed linens, so you can pick any of the three bedrooms upstairs you fancy."

"Okay." Karin headed toward the staircase.

"Look in the bathroom drawers. There are probably a couple of new toothbrushes."

"Thanks." Karin stopped at the foot of the stairs. "Do you need help?"

"No! I'm not an infant."

That had obviously been the wrong thing to ask. Dismayed, Karin watched him turn the wheelchair sharply away from her, dismissing her curtly. Karin swallowed her disappointment. For a few moments, they'd been at ease with each other. She was positive he'd enjoyed her company until she'd forgotten how supersensitive Aaron was about accepting help necessitated by his handicap. Not that he'd been in the habit of asking for help before his accident.

Starting up the stairs, she said, "Good night." Whether he heard her, she didn't know.

At the top of the stairs she paused, looking at the

hallway before her. The door at the far end stood open, revealing a bathtub, thus the three closed doors had to be bedrooms. Should she simply use the first bedroom she came to or satisfy her curiosity and look at all the rooms? It seemed like an invasion of his privacy to do this. Yet Aaron had told her to choose. How could she make a choice without looking at all of them?

Karin opened the first door. The room contained two single beds with matching dark-gold bedspreads and drapes. It was a pleasant, soothing guest room, Karin thought.

The room across the hall caused Karin's eyes to round in admiration. Since she'd only been interested in the construction of houses and their furnishings as far as their flammability was concerned, she had no idea what the style of the furniture was called, only that it was beautiful and elegant. Too elegant for someone reeking of smoke. Quickly she closed the door.

The moment she entered the last bedroom, she knew this was the room for her. It contained the furniture from Aaron's old room. Even before she turned the light on, she knew that. Perhaps she sensed a lingering aura of his presence. It had to be something like that which drew her to it. She felt at home in it. She flipped the light on.

As then, the room looked lived in. It wouldn't be offended by a little soot and smoke. The double bed had been shoved against the wall to make room for a library table heaped with books. One wall featured a large, detailed map of Chicago, the one opposite, framed photographs of turn-of-the-century firehouses. Aaron must have told the movers exactly where to place the furniture.

Karin dropped her shoulder bag on the library table before she proceeded to the bathroom for a quick shower. As usual she hand washed her bra and panties and hung them over the shower rod to dry. Then, also as usual, she dumped her smoky, sweaty jeans and tee shirt into the tub to soak before she put them into the washing machine. Too late, it occurred to her that she had nothing to sleep in. Worse, she had nothing to wear until morning. She didn't mind sleeping in the nude, but what if Aaron suddenly needed something in the night? She had to be able to leap out of bed at the first hint of trouble and that meant she had to be wearing something.

Chewing on her lip thoughtfully, she finally came to the conclusion that she had no choice but to ask Aaron for the loan of something to wear. She eyed the large bath towel. It was big enough to wind around her and covered her from under her arms to mid-thigh. While this wasn't what she'd normally choose to wear to face Aaron, it was adequate.

Downstairs Aaron listened to Karin's movements. He'd been in and out of his shower before she had turned hers on. He had tried not to think of her. He hadn't suc-ceeded, not until he had lifted himself into that torturer's contraption his therapist had brought him which worked his near-useless legs. While he exercised, the pain drove all other thoughts from his mind. But now, exhausted, sweaty, a towel slung around his neck, he was keenly aware of her again. She seemed to be searching for something. Frowning, Aaron heaved his body into his chair and wheeled himself to the bottom of the stairs.

"Karin? Do you need something? Can I help you?"

She didn't answer. Instead he heard the light, quick steps of bare feet whisper across wood. She wouldn't, he hoped for his peace of mind, come down again.

But she did. At least part of the way. Clad only in a bath towel, she stopped on the landing, poised for flight like a skittish colt. Amused, he noted that she used the newel-post as a shield.

"I'm looking for something to sleep in," Karin said.

Aaron stared at her for a second. Her hair was wet, her face free from makeup. She looked so lovely, so innocent, so young, that his breath caught.

When Aaron remained silent, she explained her predicament. "I soaked all of my clothes before I remembered that I didn't have any clean ones with me. Do you have a tee shirt or a pajama top I could wear?"

With an effort, Aaron jerked his gaze from hers. Pointing to the dining room, he said, "There's probably something in the chest in there. You'll have to come down to get it." He was careful to keep his eyes averted as she hurried down the stairs and rushed past him. He could not, however, keep from inhaling the fragrance of soap and warm woman. His hands gripped the arms of his chair.

"May I take the navy pajamas with the maroon piping?" she called to him.

"Yes." He knew his voice lacked its usual decisive quality. He hoped Karin hadn't noticed.

"Sure you won't need them tonight?" Karin asked, returning to where he'd stayed as if rooted to the floor.

"I have other pajamas." Aaron could feel her eyes on his naked torso, the brief gym shorts he wore, his bare legs. Though he knew she looked at him for only a second or two, he felt increasingly hot under her frank appraisal. When their eyes met, he knew that her appraisal was favorable. The temperature of the room seemed to shoot up another ten degrees. He'd have to adjust the air conditioning.

"Thanks for the loan," she said, her voice soft. Karin smiled at him briefly, shyly, before she slung the pajamas over her shoulders and walked up the stairs. Feeling his eyes on her back, she forced herself to walk and not to run.

She moved calmly, it seemed to him, while his body and his emotions were in turmoil. If his life had depended on it, he couldn't have moved from the spot until she disappeared from his sight. When he realized that his eyes had never wavered from her form, he muttered a number of colorful curses. Wheeling himself to the bathroom, he swung himself expertly onto the plastic chair under the shower for the second time.

He turned the water on full blast. Had it all been deliberate, her parade past him, with those long, gorgeous legs? No. Karin wasn't manipulative. He knew her well enough to be certain of that. Which made it even worse. If an innocent, spontaneous act on her part could bring him to this state, he'd hate to see what she could do if she put her mind to it.

Even though she'd gone to bed late, Karin woke early. For a moment, she was disoriented, until her gaze encountered the fire scene prints. She had slept in Aaron's bed. For a second she rubbed her cheek against his pillow. She stretched luxuriously, thoroughly. She couldn't keep from wondering what it would have been like waking up in this bed had they become lovers. The images left her breathless. Quickly she jumped out of bed. She must not speculate about such impossible things.

Wandering through the room, she looked at the prints again. She discovered that she had missed the small, framed drawing behind the armchair the night before. It was only a pencil sketch of a cat sitting next to a vase filled with daisies, almost primitive, childlike in execution, yet carefully, expensively mounted and framed. At the bottom, almost covered by the mounting material, she discovered some small printed letters which she thought might spell "Robert."

She frowned. She didn't remember seeing this drawing in his apartment, but then she hadn't had eyes for much beside Aaron. She knew Aaron hadn't been married and, he didn't have a brother. Who was Robert?

Checking the time again, Karin decided it was still early enough to go to the kitchen in search of coffee and breakfast without running into her boss. First, though, she had to wash and dry the clothes she'd left soaking in the bathtub.

Aaron had just finished shaving when he heard Karin rummaging in the kitchen. Hurriedly he slapped some aftershave lotion on his cheeks, winced at the stinging sensation, tightened the belt of his bathrobe and pushed himself toward the kitchen. He coasted to a stop in the open doorway. Karin, wearing his pajamas, was searching through one of the cupboards. Her pale blond hair hung loose down her back. Against the navy material it shimmered silvery.

The tea kettle's whistle propelled Karin toward the range to turn it off and plunged Aaron back to reality. He couldn't believe he'd just indulged himself in ogling a woman who worked for him. An arson investigator on his team. A colleague. Karin was his assistant. Nothing more. How could he have forgotten that even for a second? That burning ceiling hadn't only impaired his legs—it had obviously damaged his brain as well, he reflected disgustedly. He moved his chair into the kitchen.

Karin whirled around, startled. "I didn't hear you come down the hall. I'm making coffee. It's only instant since I couldn't find the regular. You want a cup?"

"No, thanks. Molly usually has a pot ready at the office."

"I can't wait that long. I need a cup while I get ready." Karin took a careful sip of the hot brew and grimaced. "I don't blame you for waiting till you get to work. This stuff is staler than three-day old doughnuts."

Karin opened the refrigerator and studied its contents. She stared speechlessly at the vast, white, cold emptiness. She closed it and examined the contents of the cabinet beside it. "I've seen empty cupboards before, but yours give new meaning to the words." With a frown she turned to Aaron. "What do you usually eat for breakfast?"

"Molly picks up a box of sweet rolls at the bakery each morning." His voice sounded defensive. That irritated him. First Karin distracted him at the crack of dawn and then she drove him on the defensive about his eating habits. All this had to stop right then and there. After all, theirs could only be a working relationship. Nothing more. He glowered at her. At least he tried to glower, but it was difficult when his eyes kept straying to that gorgeous hair cascading down her back.

Karin closed the cupboard. "No wonder you're so irritable. Consuming all that sugar on an empty stomach is hard on your system."

"I'm not irritable." Aaron gritted his teeth in total frustration. This wasn't going the way he had planned.

"You most certainly are, but that's okay now that I know the cause. Your body is starved for food. Good food, not a lot of worthless sugar." Karin finished her search of his kitchen.

"Will you stop swishing around?" Aaron demanded.

Karin raised a pale, finely arched eyebrow. "Swishing? I've never swished in my entire life. I'm only trying to find something to eat."

"Blast it, Karin, I'll take you out to breakfast. Just get dressed," he snapped.

"That's not the most gracious invitation I've ever received." When she saw his eyes narrow dangerously, she said, "Oh, all right. Give me ten minutes to get ready."

"Make it five."

"Seven. I have to take my clothes out of the dryer."

Chapter Five

They worked remarkably well together, Karin observed again. At the burned-out furniture store she gathered samples of accelerant-soaked material, ashes, bits of wood, plastic, masonry, electrical wiring and whatever else seemed important and carried them to Aaron who'd propelled his chair as close to the area she was investigating as possible. He labeled and dated the samples. Then he dispatched them by special messenger to the lab.

After their big breakfast both had declined to stop work for lunch. Both were acutely aware that the first twenty-four hours were critical. It was during this time that clues were contamination free; that witnesses were not only still in the area, but likely to recall important details.

It was not until mid-afternoon that Aaron asked her to stop.

"One of the men came by to report. He offered to get us something to eat." Aaron handed a paper sack to Karin. "I told him you were a vegetarian. He said a cheese sandwich and the apple was the best he could come up with in this neighborhood."

"That's fine. Sometimes I eat meat when there's nothing else available." Karin took off her gloves and helmet. She rinsed her hands with water from the plastic gallon jug they'd brought. Then she sat tailor-fashion on the sidewalk next to Aaron's wheelchair and bit heartily into the sandwich. They were silent while they ate. It was an easy silence that neither felt compelled to fill with chatter.

The August air shimmered fluidly with heat. After she'd eaten her apple, Karin raised her face toward the sun.

"You don't seem to mind the heat and the sun," Aaron remarked.

"No. Actually, I love it. Must be something that's genetically imprinted, courtesy of that long line of Nordic ancestors who lived through those endless, sunless winters." Karin glanced at Aaron. His shirt was barely wilted even though he'd been sitting in the strong light for hours. "You seem to be holding up well under the heat yourself," she said.

He shrugged. "I ignore it."

Aaron was disciplined enough to do just that, Karin

thought. With his iron will he could endure almost anything. Discipline was admirable, but it also had its downside. To Karin, the ability to ignore feelings that were inconvenient or troubling seemed like a negative trait. Sooner or later those emotions had to be dealt with and talked about. That had been their biggest problem in the past. Aaron rarely revealed what he felt. It had made her feel left out of his life. Would he have changed if they'd had more time? She had no way of knowing. The accident had wiped out any future they might have had together.

Covertly, Karin studied Aaron's face. The strong features betrayed none of the thoughts and emotions he felt. If she were foolish enough to fall for him again, she would run head on into that iron control and unyielding discipline. As long as he was in a wheelchair, he would remain as distant and as unapproachable as the burning sun above. He had told her as much in the hospital, and nothing had changed since then.

Karin clenched her hands. Even if or when he got out of that chair, she had no indication, no assurance whatsoever that he would be interested in her again. Whatever they'd had was over. A burning ceiling had ended it. She couldn't, wouldn't, be so self-destructive as to allow herself any romantic notions about Aaron. As he'd said plainly enough, they were an arson investigation team—he her boss, she his assistant. Nothing more. Or so he had claimed.

After last night she wasn't so sure of that anymore.

In that first unguarded moment when Aaron had caught sight of her standing on the steps, she'd seen desire leap into his hazel eyes. It had been that same hot, hungry look that used to turn her legs weak. For a couple of heartbeats, the attraction had sparked between them as powerfully as before the accident.

How was she to interpret that? Karin had deliberately put off thinking about last night in the hope that time might help her put Aaron's reaction in the proper perspective. The passing hours hadn't helped. She was as confused now as she'd been last night. The problem was that one unguarded reaction wasn't enough to build dreams on. If only she had some way of finding out how Aaron really felt about her.

"So, what do you think?" Aaron asked after the lengthy silence.

"Pardon?" Startled, Karin wondered if Aaron, too, had been trying to come to terms with last night.

"About this latest fire?" Aaron prompted.

"Oh." Quickly she focused on the arson. "I'm fairly sure we're dealing with the same arsonist." Karin crushed the empty paper sack between the palms of her hands.

"You found the point of origin for the second fire then."

A statement, not a question, as if he, too, had more than half expected that. Karin nodded in agreement.

"Blast! That's the third major fire he's set in four weeks. We're missing something."

"I don't see how we could be. We've investigated the two latest fires by the book," she said, her chin tilted stubbornly. "We've checked and double-checked. I swear we overlooked nothing." Karin stood up, automatically dusting off the seat of her jeans. She knew Aaron was watching her, but since his dark sunglasses hid his eyes, she had no idea what expression they held.

"I've got another hour's work." She scooped up her helmet and gloves, tossed her thick, flaxen braid over her shoulder and turned toward the burned furniture store.

"Take your time. In this case, accuracy is of the essence, not speed," Aaron said.

Heeding his admonishment, Karin triple-checked each phase of her evidence-gathering before she was satisfied and ready to return to headquarters. There, she discovered that she'd used her spare set of clothes and since she hadn't gone to her apartment the night before, she hadn't replaced them. Drat. That meant she couldn't take a shower. Well, she could take a shower, but what good would it do if she had to put the same sweat-and-smoke soaked clothes on again? Thoroughly uncomfortable and disgruntled, she slammed the door to her locker and stormed into the darkroom to develop the rolls of film she'd taken. The faster she worked, the sooner she could go home.

When Aaron joined her in the conference room where she had just finished pinning the latest photos on the board, she saw that he had showered and changed his clothes. He looked handsome. Worse, he smelled fresh and clean, while she reeked like a walking smoke-stack. Irritation and resentment surged through her.

Aaron noted her appearance and correctly interpret-ed the stormy expression in her blue-green eyes that fairly dared him to comment on her begrimed looks. Wisely he refrained. He slowly wheeled himself past the photos, studying each intently.

"So, he set two fires again, just as we thought. One in the southeast part of the building and the other in the northwest. Thorough. Thorough and clever."

Karin agreed with Aaron's assessment. How long would it take them to catch this arsonist? What if they never—no! She refused to consider the possibility of failure, but she hated to think how much damage he could do before they nabbed him.

As if he'd sensed her worries, Aaron added, "There's no arsonist so skilled that he can't be apprehended. We'll get him. It may take longer than I'd like, but we'll catch him."

Aaron's hazel eyes glittered with zeal and resolve. He harbored absolutely no doubts that they'd eventual-ly succeed, Karin realized, immensely reassured. Gratitude for his strength, his certainty, swept through her, obliterating her earlier resentment.

"Okay, let's call it a night. Drop me off at my house—unless you'd like to get something to eat first?"

"No. I'm dying to get out of these clothes and under a shower. I couldn't possibly eat until I'm clean." Her jeans could probably stand up by themselves: they were that stiff with dried sweat and grime. As for her tee shirt, it was plastered damply to her chest like a second layer of skin. Feeling his eyes upon her, she pulled at it in a futile effort to render it less formfitting.

"Then move it," he ordered, his voice brusque, carefully looking past her.

What was the matter with Aaron now? Had her refusal to eat with him upset him? Surely not. Hadn't it been a casual invitation from a coworker? Maybe not. After last night, Karin wasn't so sure of anything anymore. She stared with a puzzled expression at his retreating back. With a helpless shrug, she followed him to the van.

It wasn't until they'd reached his house that she remembered his empty refrigerator. "What'll you do for food? Do you want me to drive you to the grocery store?" she asked.

Aaron raised a dark eyebrow at her. "Bergstrom, haven't you heard of restaurants that deliver?"

"Pizza, you mean."

"It's food, isn't it? Anyway, don't worry about me. I'm not helpless."

Though Aaron's face was expressionless, Karin heard the no-trespassing note in his voice again. Every time she came close to that line he'd drawn around himself, his defense mechanism sprang into action. Heaven forbid anyone should feel compassion for him, or even plain, everyday concern. The accident had intensified his natural emotional guardedness. He was as bristly as a porcupine.

"If you don't need me anymore—" Aaron's cell phone interrupted her sentence.

Aaron listened intently. From his terse replies, she gathered that another fire had been reported. She unfolded the south Chicago map she kept on the seat beside her.

Leaning forward, Aaron pointed to a location on the map. When he replaced the receiver, he said, "It could be our arsonist again."

"Two nights in a row?" Karin asked.

"I know that's unusual, but we can't take a chance. If it's his fire, we need to be there."

Karin refolded the map.

"I told you this wasn't going to be easy when you took the job."

"Did I say anything?" she demanded, shooting him a severe look.

"No, you didn't," Aaron admitted.

The note of approval in his voice and the grin he flashed her made Karin forget that she'd felt grimy and miserable only seconds earlier.

Five hours later Karin once again parked the van behind Aaron's house. Dazed with fatigue, it seemed as if she'd repeated this maneuver countless times before. She felt as if she stood outside her own body, observing. Everything appeared unreal even though she knew it was real enough. God, she was tired. Tired all the way to her bone marrow. Karin fought the impulse to close her eyes and let go.

"Are you okay?" Aaron asked.

His voiced acted like an electric prod, causing her to sit up straight. "Of course, I'm okay," she mumbled. Karin opened the door of the van and slid out. The hot, humid air wrapped itself around her like a heavy, wet bath towel.

"There's no 'of course' about it. You're exhausted. You need to hit the sack immediately, not spend another forty-five minutes driving to your apartment. You're spending the night with me and tomorrow you're moving into my house."

"What?" Karin's voice sounded like a frog's croaking.

"You heard me."

Karin shook her head obstinately. "I can't do that."

"Hand me your car keys. You're too tired to drive." When she hesitated, Aaron gripped her wrist. "Now, Karin. I won't be responsible for you wrapping your car around the nearest tree or crashing it into a building."

"You're the bossiest, most aggravating man I've ever met."

"I know, you've told me that once or twice in the past."

"It didn't make much of an impression on you, did it?" she muttered.

Though he tried, Aaron couldn't quite repress the grin tugging at his mouth. "Karin, don't fight me on this. You won't win."

He was right. She was too tired to drive home and she didn't have the strength to fight him. Though she hated doing it, she handed him her keys.

"Thank you. You can use the same bed you had last night and the pajamas."

He led the way to the back porch as if everything were settled. It wasn't, but Karin couldn't think of a convincing argument against spending the night in his upstairs bedroom. A little resentful of the high-handed manner in which he took over, she said, "Okay, I'll take you up on your offer to spend the night. I'm sure my roommate won't mind bringing me a change of clothes in the morning."

"Good."

"But I can't possibly move in with you, so you can just forget that idea."

"Why can't you move in with me?" he challenged.

There were a dozen reasons why she couldn't live in his house. No, actually just one. It would be too hard to be with Aaron twenty-four hours a day. It was difficult enough to be close to him at work, but sharing the same living space would be pure agony. Naturally she couldn't tell him that.

What *was* she going to tell him? She was far from sure that in the intimate atmosphere of shared living quarters she could retain that objective, cool, profes-sional attitude she strove for at work. What if she unin-tentionally revealed those softer emotions she felt for him, like compassion and caring, that she couldn't root out of her heart no matter how hard she tried? He would hate her for them. As long as he was in that wheelchair, he wanted nothing from her but her professional expertise.

"Well, why can't you move into my house?" he repeated.

"It's not seemly."

Aaron whipped the wheelchair around so fast Karin almost landed in his lap. "Not seemly?" he repeated as if he hadn't heard her correctly. "*Seemly?* Now I *know* how really tired you are. The Karin I'm familiar with wouldn't be caught dead using an archaic word like 'seemly'." Shaking his head, he pushed the wheel to put the chair into motion again.

He was right, she admitted bleakly. She couldn't imagine what had prompted her to use that old-fashioned term. Her mind raced to come up with irrefutable reasons why she couldn't live with him. Suddenly she found them.

"Never mind the unseemliness of what you're demanding," she said, following him into the house. "There are, however, a number of practical reasons why I can't move in with you. Such as the fact that I signed a lease. I can't break it, and I can't afford rent on two places." *There, that should convince him*, Karin thought triumphantly.

"Did I ask you to pay rent?"

"Well, no," she conceded with a frown.

"As you'll recall," Aaron said in an exaggeratedly

patient voice, "my initial plan was for my assistant to move in upstairs. I was right in thinking that the best, most efficient arrangement. I'm going back to that plan. If we're going to put a dent in the arson cases already on file and maybe, just maybe discourage a few torches from setting future fires in my district, we have to be smarter, faster, craftier and more efficient than any arsonist alive."

Aaron paused to take a breath. Before Karin could say anything, he continued.

"I can't have an assistant who spends precious time commuting to a room to sleep in. Face it, Karin. That's all you've been using your apartment for anyway. You can sleep just as well upstairs. It's that or I'll have to find myself an assistant willing to live on the premises. I don't really want a different assistant because I've trained you, you're excellent at your job, I'm used to you, and we get along. So the choice is up to you. I'll expect your answer in the morning."

Karin stood speechlessly in the hall, watching Aaron wheel himself into his converted bedroom. A moment later, he appeared in the doorway.

"Catch," he called, tossing a white terry cloth robe at her."

"Thanks."

"Good night," Aaron said and closed the door behind him.

For another few seconds she stood there, clutching the robe, too stunned to move.

Aaron had actually said that she did a good job. That he was used to her. That they got along well. He had never said this many positive things about her in all the time they'd known each other.

This was almost too much to take in. She roused herself from her bemused state. There was so much to think about she didn't know where to begin. And she was tired. Too tired to make the major decisions about moving in with him. That would have to wait until morning. Holding onto the banister, she dragged herself upstairs.

Karin resisted the annoying noise that pierced her sleep, but despite her best efforts, it eventually roused her. Her hand groped for the button on the alarm clock, only to find it already pushed down. Had she forgotten to set it? Dismayed, she sat up to look at the clock.

"Oh no!" Nine o'clock. She should have been at the office an hour ago. The ringing noise persisted. Perhaps it was the telephone, she thought groggily. She remembered seeing one in the hallway. Grabbing the robe Aaron had given her, she dashed out of the room. It wasn't the phone. All she got was the dial tone when she picked up the receiver.

"Doorbell," she muttered. Shrugging into the robe, she padded swiftly on bare feet down the stairs.

"Aaron?" she called. The door to his room was open. His narrow hospital bed was neatly made. Where was he? "Aaron?" she called again over the din of the doorbell. Whoever was out there must be keeping a finger on the button, Karin thought resentfully. "Aaron?" No answer. She hated to answer his door dressed the way she was but the persistence of the visitor left her no choice. Opening the door, she came face-to-face with her roommate.

"Alice, what in the world are you doing? How did you know I was here?"

"Aaron phoned me an hour ago."

"He did. Why?"

"To bring you some clean clothes. May I come in?"

"Of course." Karin stepped aside to allow Alice to enter. More to herself she muttered, "I wonder where Aaron is. Probably already at the office, preparing a lecture on the sins of oversleeping."

"Sweetpea, it's Sunday morning. Nobody goes to the office on Sunday mornings."

"Ha! That's what you think. Aaron does and probably already has."

"Nope. I met him outside a few minutes ago. His cousin is taking him to physical therapy. Those Knights sure are a pair of hunks," Alice said, an appreciative gleam in her eyes.

Karin felt an immense load lift off her chest. She wouldn't have to face Aaron about oversleeping. Darn, how she hated falling short of his expectations. Rubbing her left temple, she murmured, "I need coffee."

"You look like death warmed over. If I didn't know better I'd say you had a hangover," Alice remarked.

"If there's such a thing as a lack-of-sleep hangover, then I've got a doozy."

"Speaking of coffee, Aaron said to bring some since he had only instant, which you hate." Pulling a package from the large bag she was carrying, Alice said, "So here's a pound of dark roasted Colombian beans, freshly ground, just the way you like them."

"Bless you. You're a lifesaver." Karin hugged her roommate. Then clutching the bag possessively to her chest, she hurried to the kitchen.

Alice followed and watched Karin's ritualistic coffee making with amused tolerance. "You're going to brew a whole pot?" she finally asked.

"You bet. Even if you don't want any, the way I feel, I can kill the whole pot by myself." Karin poured water into the coffee maker, but instead of placing the pot underneath to catch the dark liquid, she set her mug there. With both elbows on the kitchen counter, she leaned down to watch the process and to inhale the tantalizing aroma. When the mug was full, she smoothly slid the glass pot into its place.

"I'm always amazed at how well you do that. You never spill a drop," Alice remarked.

"Practice. I can never wait until the whole pot is done." Karin took that first sip and closed her eyes in bliss. She finished half the mug before she spoke. "I don't know how Aaron does it. He's had as little sleep as I have and there he's off to a therapy session which is bound to be strenuous."

"Motivation. If you want something bad enough, you'll do most anything to get it."

Karin nodded in agreement. She couldn't imagine Aaron wanting anything more desperately than getting out of that wheelchair.

"Speaking of Aaron, he also said to bring you breakfast since there was no food in the house. So I stopped at the bakery to pick up half a dozen of your favorite cranberry-walnut muffins and at the grocery store for juice, milk and cereal. What do you want to eat first?"

"Everything," Karin said, quickly reaching for plates, bowls and spoons. "We didn't get any dinner last night. The glasses are in the cupboard above the sink."

Alice went to fetch them. "That's some life you're leading these days. Little sleep and no food."

"Tell me about it. Can you believe that I forgot to set the alarm clock last night? I've never, ever done that in my entire life."

"I know. You usually set two." Alice waited until Karin had slaked her hunger before she spoke again. "I never see you anymore. You creep in during the middle of the night and drag yourself out at the crack of dawn. Never mind about me, but that poor cat you adopted is freaking out. When he isn't chewing on the ribbons of your nightgown he walks around yowling fit to break your heart."

Karin put her spoon down. "I'm sorry. I didn't think it was going to be this bad, but arson is one of the fastest growing crimes around, and Aaron and I are determined to do something about it."

"But how long can you keep up this pace?"

"That's the problem. I'm spending too much time commuting. Aaron delivered an ultimatum last night: move in upstairs or he'll replace me with an assistant who won't hesitate about sharing his house."

"Now that's what I call an ultimatum," Alice said, impressed. She reached for a muffin. Catching her roommate's eye, she said, "Oh, the heck with my diet." Between bites she asked, "What are you going to do about this ultimatum?"

Karin sighed. "What can I do? I'm back in the same position I was in three weeks ago. No, actually it's worse," she amended. "If I quit now, everybody will be convinced it's because I couldn't get along with a pre-dominately male team and that'll finish me profession-ally. This is practically an all-male occupation. I can count the female arson investigators in this city on my fingers. The men in this field would sooner forgive me for being incompetent, showing up drunk, or having a lousy work ethic than for not being able to be a team player."

"Then you have no choice but to move in with Aaron."

"I was afraid that was the only choice I had so I hadn't put it into words yet."

"What are you afraid of?"

Karin lifted her hands and her shoulders and then dropped both of them in a gesture signaling confusion.

"You've never particularly cared about what people said or thought of you in the past, so that can't be the reason." Alice studied Karin's face. Softly, she asked, "Are you afraid you might be falling in love with Aaron again?"

Karin felt the blood rush to her head. It pounded in her ears like ocean waves crashing against rocks at high tide. "I'm not falling in love with Aaron. Absolutely not! Do you think I'm completely insane? Or self-destructive?"

Alice continued to study Karin.

"I'm neither! The last thing on earth I want to do is fall in love with Aaron Knight!"

"Sometimes we have no control over our hearts."

Karin's shoulders slumped. "That's true, but I can't allow myself to love him. He told me straight out in the hospital that as long as he's in a wheelchair, there's no chance for us."

"That was then. Almost two years have passed. He might have changed his mind. Or he might change it in the future."

"I don't know. Aaron is very stubborn. I don't think he breaks resolutions he's made." She stared thoughtfully into her coffee cup before she spoke again. "Aaron getting out of the wheelchair isn't the real issue. It may be for him, but not for me."

"Don't you think I know that? You're not the kind of woman who'd abandon a man in his hour of need."

"That's just it. Aaron doesn't *want* to need anybody.

He never has. Sometimes I think he's afraid to let himself need anyone. Especially a woman. To need someone is to open yourself to rejection and pain."

Alice nodded. "Do you have any idea why he feels that way?"

Karin sighed and shook her head.

Alice studied Karin for several seconds. "There's something else, isn't there?"

Karin closed her eyes in despair. "I keep remembering the argument we had before the accident."

"Stop right there. We've talked about this before. You're not responsible for that ceiling collapsing."

"But Aaron was upset when he left me. Our argument could have caused him to be less careful than he usually is."

"You read the report. Did it say he'd been careless?"

"Well, no. Still. I'll always wonder."

"Have you asked him if he blames you?"

"In the hospital—"

"I mean recently."

"No."

"Maybe you should."

They were silent for several minutes. Finally Alice spoke. "Karin, will moving in with him change how you feel?"

"Probably not, but I can't be sure."

"What are you afraid of?" Alice asked.

"That if I move in, I might not be able to keep from wanting to do things for him. You know, like jumping up to fetch stuff for him, open doors, ask him if he's in pain, if he needs anything. Aaron hates that. It makes him feel worse about being unable to walk than he already does. I've been able to control it at work, but I'm not sure I can keep myself from doing it if we're together for twenty-four hours a day."

Alice's voice was very soft when she asked, "Karin, has it occurred to you that you're not falling in love with Aaron because you never stopped loving him?"

Karin sat completely still for several seconds. When she spoke her voice resonated with pain. "He told me to get out of his life. It just about broke my heart. How could I possibly still be in love with him?"

"That, I suspect, is only a rhetorical question."

Karin shook her head in denial—and to clear it of memories and emotions.

"Besides, it doesn't matter how I feel about him. I work with him every day, so I must be in control. I must be objective. I must remind myself that Aaron doesn't need or want help no matter what. I must be professional at all times."

"That's a tall order," Alice said with compassion.

"I know. Pray that I'm up to it." Karin took a shuddering breath. She faced Alice with a small, brave smile. "So, are you going to help me move my stuff?" Karin asked, her voice bright, skimming over the doubts and fears that tore her apart.

Chapter Six

"**K**arin? There's a big black-and-white cat lying in the middle of my bed," Aaron yelled from the foot of the stairs. He hoped the noise he heard of objects being pushed around was Karin moving her things into his house. He'd allowed her plenty of time since the arrival of Alice before he'd returned.

"That's Vulcan. I wondered where he'd gotten to. I told him to stay up here, but he's not into total obedience."

"Just like you."

"I heard that. Is that any way to talk to your new housemate?"

Relief flooded through Aaron. She *had* moved in. When he found himself grinning like an idiot, he realized that the relief was tinged with a good deal of joy.

That sobered him quickly. His reaction, he assured himself, was due to the fact that now he wouldn't have to train a new assistant who wouldn't be nearly as good as Karin. She would continue to be part of his team, a team that had a real chance of cleaning up the arson mess in his district.

Karin appeared at the top of the stairs and Aaron's jaw dropped open. When he'd insisted she move in with him, he'd thought he would see her only as she was dressed for work: in jeans that covered her legs and loose shirts that merely hinted at the curves beneath. But that sexy woman skipping lightly down the steps wore a sleeveless, vee-necked tee shirt that clung to her torso and a pair of white shorts that displayed every inch of her magnificent legs. He swallowed hard. He hadn't counted on that. Something in his expression must have betrayed him, for Karin launched into an explanation.

"I hadn't planned on wearing anything quite this informal, but it's too hot and stuffy upstairs." She tucked a damp strand of hair behind her ear that had escaped her ponytail.

Now Aaron noted a sheen of perspiration on her forehead, her throat. Before he knew what was happening, he found himself breaking out in perspiration all over, too. He was aware of the real reason for the heat he felt coursing through his entire body. It wasn't all due to the temperature in the house, not by a long shot.

He'd have to do better in the future. He couldn't

allow himself to react to Karin like a lover. He'd have to be on guard. Today she'd caught him unawares, but in the future that shouldn't happen again. *Couldn't* happen again. Raising his arm to wipe the sweat on his forehead against the sleeves of his shirt, he pulled himself together.

"It *is* hot in here," he finally managed to say. "The air conditioner must be on the blink," he said.

"It is. I checked. All it does is blow the warm air around."

"Great. We'll never get a repair man to come on a Sunday afternoon."

"Probably not. I noticed the leaves on the trees moving. We'd be better off opening all the windows to catch whatever breeze there is, don't you agree?"

"Yes. Why don't you open the ones upstairs? I'll get the windows down here," Aaron suggested.

"Okay."

With an effort Aaron turned away to prove to himself that he could. He wouldn't ogle Karin. Except turning away didn't do much good. In his mind's eye, he knew exactly what her long legs looked like hurrying up the stairs. Aaron ground his teeth. Then with more force than necessary, he opened the windows. At least all the ones he could reach. He was sitting in front of the high hall window that was too far up on the wall for him to get to when Karin rejoined him.

"It would provide some cross ventilation if I opened it, don't you think?" she asked.

Without waiting for him to move, Karin reached over to open the window. Her hip brushed against his arm. The impact of her touch slammed through Aaron, all the way down to his injured legs. He knew he should move, should break the physical contact, yet he sat as if his chair had been nailed to the floor boards.

Some time that day she had put on that lotion she wore which he'd come to associate with her. It reminded him of the sweet scent of flowers on a hot summer night. And of something else, something less innocent than flowers, something darker, headier, with a hint of fire and danger.

Without thinking, Aaron grabbed Karin's hand. He pressed it against his cheek. He had meant to stop with this small gesture of . . . gratitude, but her scent, the feel of her skin, overwhelmed him. He had to taste her just one more time. Turning his head slightly, he kissed the soft inside of her wrist. He felt her pulse race, felt it leap into him, engulf him like a wall of fire. The pleasure coursing through him was so intense it was as much agony as it was joy. Through the pounding of his wild blood he heard a soft moan. He didn't know if he'd uttered the sound, but it broke the spell.

Karin snatched her hand from his grip, yet she didn't move away. For a moment they remained as if frozen in time and space. Then she stepped back.

"There. That should do it," Karin said, her voice whispery.

Aaron cleared his throat. "The carpenter who put up

the ramps and made other adjustments necessary for the wheelchair, offered to rig a contraption so I could open the high windows, but I told him it wasn't necessary since I didn't plan to be in this lousy chair that long."

"Makes sense," Karin murmured. She followed Aaron down the hall as if in a trance.

They stopped in the doorway to Aaron's room. Vulcan was reclining in the middle of the bed like some eastern potentate. Through slitted, yellow eyes he watched the man in the wheelchair.

"You named your cat after the Roman god of fire?" Aaron asked with a raised eyebrow.

"Why not? He does look sort of majestic, doesn't he?" Without waiting for Aaron's reply, she continued. "You're not allergic to cats, are you?"

"No."

"Good. Afraid of them?"

"Hardly."

"Great," Karin said, smiling in relief. "Because where I go, my cat goes, too. We're a set."

Seeing the determined angle of her chin, Aaron hastened to reassure her. "I have no objections to Vulcan, provided he doesn't take over my bed."

"He won't. He usually sleeps with me."

Lucky cat, Aaron couldn't prevent himself from thinking.

Vulcan, as if he knew he wasn't wanted on the bed, stood up, stretched leisurely, hopped off the bed and rubbed himself against Karin's bare legs.

A very lucky cat, Aaron added silently.

"I had started to fix a pasta dish for dinner," Karin said, "but it's too hot, so I'll turn it into a cold pasta salad, if you don't mind."

"I don't mind at all. Karin, you moving in doesn't mean you have to turn into my housekeeper."

"I hadn't planned on it, but I do like to eat and all you have in your freezer are TV dinners." Karin shuddered delicately. "I'll do the cooking." With that pronouncement, she fled toward the kitchen.

For a tall, well-muscled woman, she walked with uncommon grace, Aaron observed once again appreciatively. Her movements were fluid, loose-limbed like a dancer's or a gymnast's. It was a pleasure to watch her move. When he caught himself zeroing in on that seductive sway of her hips, Aaron brought himself up short.

"Fool," he muttered to himself. He was still confined to that miserable wheelchair and had no business hungering for Karin. Until he could stand on two strong legs, she was off limits.

Bright and early on Monday morning, they resumed work. Even though Karin had stayed up late getting settled in, the time she'd spent commuting now gave her the extra sleep she needed to feel strong and fit.

Since Aaron, as he put it, "had to waste his time" in a monthly meeting with directors of other arson units, he'd assigned Simon as her partner to investigate the

Saturday night fire. Aaron seemed unusually preoccupied that morning, as he'd been the evening before.

Dinner on Sunday night had been a fairly silent affair. Immediately after their after-dinner coffee Aaron had excused himself to work on a report for Monday's meeting. She hadn't seen him again that evening. She told him good night through the closed door of his room. She knew that the less she saw of Aaron at his house, the easier their cohabitation would be. Yet deep down she'd been disappointed that he hadn't opened his door to bid her good night.

Simon volunteered to take the photographs of the fire-damaged duplex, leaving Karin to gather and record samples. They worked silently, efficiently. They were done by noon.

While Simon developed the photos, Karin showered in the cubicle that had been rigged up for her. Using the type of plywood sheets commonly nailed over burned out windows and doors, the workmen had partitioned off part of the shower room. She now had privacy and a door that locked.

Karin dressed in the tailored oyster-white linen slacks and matching tunic she kept in the locker for interviews with witnesses and potential arsonists. While taking samples, she'd found that the blown-out back door of the downstairs apartment had kept bothering her. She had to take another look at it.

When she returned a couple of hours later, Molly waylaid her.

"Aaron told me he wanted to see you the minute you got back," the secretary informed her.

"Oh. What's up?"

Molly shrugged. "I think he's anxious to hear about the Saturday fire."

Karin knocked on Aaron's office door before entering.

"Where have you been?" he demanded without preamble.

"Following up a hunch."

"From that satisfied expression on your face, the hunch must have paid off. Well?"

"Have you looked at the pictures Simon took this morning?"

"Last time I checked he hadn't posted them yet in the conference room." Aaron wheeled himself around his desk. "Let's go and take a look at them."

Karin followed Aaron down the hall. He was still wearing the dove gray suit he'd worn to the meeting. He looked so good Karin kept stealing glances at him.

They found the stack of photos on the desk with a note saying Simon would display them as soon as he got back from the latest fire.

"Was this fire set by our arsonist?" Aaron asked while Karin pinned the photos to the board.

"No. There was only one point of origin."

"It's unlikely, but he might have thought he didn't need two starter fires since this was a smaller house."

"It's not only unlikely, it's impossible. He didn't do it."

"You look mighty cocky. What makes you so sure?"

"Would a signed confession be enough to justify my cockiness?" she asked with an impish grin. Karin loved his surprised expression.

"A signed confession? Start at the beginning and don't leave anything out." For emphasis he lifted his right index finger, but whatever small threat this gesture might have had, was undermined by the smile lifting the corners of his mouth.

Karin handed him a photo. "As you can see from this, at first it looked like an electrical fire. And those, as you know, are most often accidental fires, not arson."

"What made you suspicious that this wasn't an accidental fire?"

"The back door." Karin handed him another photo. "Look at it. From the hinges you can see that there was an explosion in the hallway just in front of the door. I figure the arsonist threw a lighted match at the accelerant he'd poured all over the floor. The charring pattern suggests that he miscalculated the speed with which the fire spread. There's no way he could have gotten away quickly enough to escape injuries."

Aaron nodded, impressed. "Unless he was an Olympic sprinter, the force that blew the door would have propelled it far enough to catch him in the back."

"That's what I figured, too, so I phoned every emergency room within a five-mile radius of the duplex."

"And?"

"And there were three admissions on Saturday night with serious burn wounds. One was a five-year old with hot-water burns. The second burn victim was a woman. Yes, I know women set fires, too, but not very often, so I decided to check her after the third victim, if he wasn't the right one. He was, though."

"Go on."

"He was smart enough to use an alias at the hospital, but dumb enough, or in enough pain to be muddled when asked his address. He gave the correct one which happens to be the apartment above the one put on fire. I bluffed and told him we had irrefutable evidence that he'd set the fire. When I asked him how much he got paid for burning the house, he admitted to two-hundred-and-fifty dollars."

"That's all?"

Karin nodded. "I informed him that he got cheated. The usual fee for a fire like his was around a thousand dollars. That really made him mad. He blew his top and told me that it was his cheap, no-good, son-of-a-so-and-so landlord who hired him to torch the duplex for the insurance money. All this he spilled in the presence of two nurses who signed the confession as witnesses."

"Good job! I'll get arrest warrants for the arsonist and his landlord. That's how I like to see a case solved: fast, clean, unimpeachable. Great work, Karin."

Aaron's praise spread a warm, heady glow through Karin. It made her feel so good her feet performed a little victory shuffle on her way back to her desk.

*   *   *

Karin's euphoria lasted until she reviewed the cases set by their two-point-of-origin torch. With him they were getting nowhere fast. All the owners of the burned properties seemed to have no reason to want their buildings torched. The low-rent, single-room occupancy hotels were actually underinsured. That left the owners of the furniture store. It was time to speak to them.

Aaron was in another meeting.

"He's bound to be in that one the rest of the afternoon. It's a budget conference." Molly grimaced. "They usually last long, are unsatisfactory, and leave the boss man in a depressed mood."

"Tell him I went to interview the Knolls. I should be back by six. Maybe I'll have good news to cheer him up."

Karin talked to the owners of the incinerated furniture store. When she left them, she was convinced that they weren't responsible for the fire. Thinking about their loss, she muttered, "You, Mr. Two-Point, have a lot to answer for."

On the way back, she remembered that there was nothing to eat at Aaron's place except a couple of frozen dinners. The mere thought of them gave her indigestion. Since Aaron would be in a meeting all afternoon, he wouldn't miss her for another hour or so.

Karin's plan worked. She got back to the office in plenty of time to type up her report of the Knoll interview.

Aaron's meeting ran late. After he'd checked his messages, he declared himself ready to go home. That surprised Karin into silence. It was barely 6:00. They never left the office before 7:00. In the van, she kept glancing anxiously at him in the rearview mirror. He looked exhausted, as if he'd been in a battle all day. Alarmed, she studied his face, his posture. Surely it wasn't good for him to work this hard. Hadn't his doctor warned him against that?

Of course he had, but that didn't mean Aaron would follow his doctor's advice. She knew him well enough to know that. To whom did men listen? Their mothers, their wives, their sweethearts. Since she qualified as none of those, she should keep her nagging to herself and her mouth shut, but Karin found she couldn't do that. As a coworker she had the right to ask pertinent, sympathetic questions, didn't she?

"You look like you've been through the proverbial wringer today," Karin commented.

Aaron looked up from the report he'd been reading. His expression was surprised when their glances met in the rearview mirror.

"Those budget meetings are like hand-to-hand combat with each director trying to win as much for his department as he can."

Karin was dying to ask how he'd come out of the skirmish but realized the question was out of line. As if he sensed her curiosity, he told her.

"We may, and I stress *may*, get two more arson investigators. Molly put together some statistics which glaringly demonstrated our need for more manpower. I hadn't realized that every investigator put in at least a sixty-hour week since the department was created. That shows how dedicated my team is but no one can sustain that kind of pace indefinitely."

Not even you, she added silently.

"Some, like you, have put in more like eighty-hour weeks," Aaron said.

"And you, too."

Aaron made a dismissing motion with his hand. "That doesn't count. I'm the boss, but I had no right to ask that kind of commitment of you. The least I can do is offer you some comp time."

"Thanks, and now that you mention it, I'm going to use some comp time for tomorrow night. Several weeks ago, I promised to go to a banquet that some civic organization my friend belongs to sponsors. I need to be home, that is, at your house, by seven so I can get ready for the banquet at eight. Is that okay?"

"Sure." Aaron bent his head over the folder in his lap. Very casually he asked, "Who's the friend?"

"Jason."

"I thought your relationship with him wasn't serious."

"It isn't a 'relationship'. We're friends. I told you that. I also told you that if neither of us had a date and we had to attend a wedding, or a banquet, or some other function where we needed an escort, we went together. I promised to go to this banquet with him. Why do you find it impossible to believe that he and I can just be friends?"

Because he himself could never just be friends with Karin. Aaron could be her boss and her coworker since these roles were formal and clearly defined, but friendship? He was certain that he couldn't handle the casual affection involved in friendship—not when he felt this strong sexual pull for her. How could Jason not find Karin physically irresistible? How could he look at her and not desire her? Aaron found that notion inconceivable.

When Aaron didn't answer her question, Karin studied his face. The brooding expression discouraged further discussion.

Neither spoke until they'd reached the house. As soon as they were inside the kitchen, Aaron loosened his tie and pulled it off with a sigh of relief. He looked unutterably weary. Karin longed to stroke his brow, to touch his shoulders which were tight with tension, to place a soft kiss on those strain lines beside his mouth. She couldn't believe she was contemplating doing that! Those were the impulses of a wife greeting her tired mate at the end of a long day. *You're not his wife, so knock it off.* With that admonition to herself, she quickly shoved her hands into the pockets of her slacks and stepped away from him.

"Is there any of that ice tea left you made last night?" Aaron asked.

"I think so."

When Aaron opened the refrigerator, he stared at its

contents in surprise. "Great Scot! What's all this?" he finally asked.

"Groceries," Karin said. "I realize that's sort of an alien concept to you, but most people in this country stock their refrigerators with groceries."

His mouth quirked in amusement as he looked at Karin over his shoulder. "Groceries, huh? Now I seem to recall that concept. But, good grief, Karin, what are all those bottles doing in here? Do you expect a drought?"

"You've discovered my one secret vice. I don't smoke because heaven knows we inhale enough on the job, and I don't drink alcohol because I want to be clear-minded when I get a fire call. . . ." she shrugged, just a little embarrassed.

"So you drink mineral water? And strange fruit juices like guava and kiwi?"

That made her sound as exciting and mysterious as Pollyanna sitting on the front porch, listening to the leaves rustle. Quickly, to keep him from thinking about her dull habit, she said, "Mixed together, they taste absolutely delicious. Let me fix you one of my special concoctions."

Aaron reached out to grab her hand to stop her. "Do you know how rare it is to find a woman with as innocent a vice as that?"

Karin glanced at him to see if he was teasing her. He wasn't. His eyes locked with hers, their expression warm, approving. She felt her blood roil swiftly, excitedly through her veins. Conscious of her hand captured by his, her breath grew shallow and her lips parted slightly, invitingly. Aaron's hand tightened around hers. For a split second, she thought he would pull her into his lap to kiss her. Her heart turned a triple somersault before it knocked so hard against her ribs that she thought they'd crack. Unconsciously, she leaned slightly toward him, but the movement was enough for reality to hit.

Aaron dropped her hand as if it had turned into a live flame. Wheeling himself away, he said, "By all means. Fix me one of your concoctions."

Karin faced the open refrigerator, not wanting Aaron to see the acute disappointment that rushed through her. Rationally, she knew it was good that he'd had the strength to pull back, but emotionally she felt cheated. She'd desperately wanted him to kiss her, wanted it so badly that she now hurt all over. Blast his strength and iron will! Karin knew this was an irrational wish, but she couldn't help thinking it.

"How about kiwi?" Aaron said to break the charged silence.

"How about passion fruit?" Karin ground out. *You're so blasted disciplined; you could use some.*

"Passion . . . fruit? Now there's a heck of an idea," he remarked softly.

When she turned around, bottles in hand, she met his gaze. It was too dusky in the kitchen to see clearly, yet

Karin thought she saw a gleam in those yellow cat-eyes of his.

When Aaron turned the overhead kitchen light on, Karin blinked, feeling momentarily blinded. But then she was sort of emotionally blinded and mixed up around him anyway, she reflected bitterly. With her back to him, she filled two glasses with equal amounts of fruit juice, sparkling mineral water and ice cubes and stirred briefly. She handed one of the drinks to him.

"Thanks." He took a cautious sip. Pleasantly surprised, he drained half the glass. "This passion fruit juice is very tasty."

"I'm glad you like it," Karin said, her voice tight. She clutched the edge of the sink and stared out the small window above it. She seethed with resentment. Not so much with resentment toward Aaron, she discovered, as with resentment toward herself. What was the matter with her? She should be grateful that Aaron had had the presence of mind, the strength, to prevent that kiss. One kiss wouldn't have satisfied her now anymore than it had in the past. Most likely that one kiss would have led to another and still another until she was weak-kneed and breathless. Where would that have left them? Uneasy with each other, that fragile web of carefully cultivated civilized behavior they'd forged torn beyond repair, their working relationship endangered.

Aaron hadn't asked her to come back into his life. She'd been forced into it. How could she forget that even for an instant? And what in heaven's name had prompted her to think of the past, of the kisses, of what had been between them? The past was dead. It had died that day in the hospital. The present was frozen in a precarious working relationship. The future was uncertain at best. None of this bore dwelling on, not unless she wanted to drive herself crazy. She didn't. Karin took a deep breath, held it, and released it slowly. Behind her she heard the rustling of paper. She took another calming breath.

"You're convinced the Knolls didn't hire our arsonist?" Aaron asked.

"Yes. The loss of the family business affected them deeply." Karin turned around. She focused on a point behind Aaron, carefully avoiding his eyes.

"Anything in the real estate angle you mention in here?"

"I considered it, but the man who wanted to buy the Knoll property wasn't insistent enough. I've never heard of a coerced sale where the prospective buyer gave up after one inquiry and immediately resorted to drastic measures," she said.

"I haven't either. The usual pattern consists of several visits with escalating threats."

"That brings me to the weakest aspect in our case: Two-Point has no motive. At least, none we've been able to discover."

"Two-Point?" Aaron asked, an amused note in his voice.

Karin shrugged. "We have to call him something."

"Two-Point," Aaron repeated, trying the name. "I like that. It suits him." He reshuffled the papers before replacing them in the folder. "We've ruled out him being the ordinary, garden-variety kind of pyromaniac because he's too methodical, too professional."

"Which means he's a hired torch. But we don't know who hired him or why." Karin sighed.

"When we know the why, we'll know the who."

"Whenever that will be."

"Sooner than you think," Aaron said. "The other arson divisions agreed to loan us some of their investigators so we can stake out Two-Point's targeted neighborhood and catch him in the act."

"That's wonderful! If we get enough investigators, we can divide into teams and cover likely target buildings. It would only have to be for three or four hours each night. From his past fires we know he sets them sometime between eight and midnight. We'll get him yet!"

Aaron smiled at Karin's enthusiasm. How lovely she was with her eyes shining and her face animated. How completely captivating and enchanting. He'd forgotten that about her. His smile died on his lips. No, he hadn't forgotten. He'd merely suppressed the memory which is what he needed to do again. And get away from her. Now. Fast.

He'd nearly succumbed to temptation a little while ago. He'd almost grabbed her, pulled her into his lap to kiss her senseless and satisfy the hunger that raged in his soul. If he had done that, what then? Sweep her into his arms and carry her to bed? Right! He couldn't even carry himself to bed on his own two feet. The reminder of his condition hit him with a devastating blow. He was a cripple confined to a wheelchair. Karin deserved better than that. Much better.

Getting back on his feet wasn't the only problem between them. He knew that. He remembered every word, every accusation she'd hurled at him during their argument on the night of his accident. He'd thought often about their relationship. He hadn't been able to keep himself from it during his long convalescence. Still, as long as he was a cripple, he couldn't even begin to work on those problems. He had to get on his feet first.

Gripping the arms of the chair, Aaron fought the wave of depression that swept over him. His doctor had said that periodic mood swings were to be expected. Maybe expected, he thought, gritting his teeth, but not tolerated. Nor would he tolerate being in this damned wheelchair forever either.

Wheeling himself toward the door, Aaron said, "I'm going to work out on my machine for a couple of hours."

Chapter Seven

Karin spent the next day pounding the pavement, trying to find witnesses to the furniture store arson. She didn't find any. That didn't surprise her, since this wasn't the kind of neighborhood where responsible citizens lingered in the streets after dark. The types who did linger wouldn't spit on an arson investigator if she were on fire. Her profession was too close to being like that of a cop's.

For her efforts she discovered one thing. Three different people had told her that they'd seen a dark-colored van, possibly navy or maroon or dark brown, cruise through the street around 8:30. They'd never seen that van before.

Back at the office Karin checked the reports of Two-

Point's previous fires. No one had reported a van, dark-colored or otherwise.

"Oh rats," she said, slamming the folder shut.

"Problems?" Aaron inquired from the door.

His voice soothed her frazzled nerves like a warm, sweet tonic. She turned to look at him. "Not even problems. Nothing. I spent the entire day knocking on doors and all I have to show for it are hot, aching feet and a slightly sunburned nose. I hate days like this. What a waste."

"Frustrating, but not a waste. Every time something is eliminated, it clears the path toward solving the case."

"I know, but it's such a negative activity. I want to discover something that'll lead straight to the arsonist."

"We all do."

"Did the other investigators come up with anything useful?"

"No. We've hit the low point. Every case has a nadir where nothing seems to be happening."

"How do we get out of this low point?"

"We get a break."

"We do? What kind of a break?"

"That's hard to predict. Every case is different. But it'll happen. Trust me on this."

Aaron was convinced of this and Karin took new courage from his certainty. "I'm sorry. I didn't meant to take out my frustration on you."

"It's okay. There's no one else here, is there?"

"No." Karin was appalled. How could she have dumped on Aaron? He was her boss, for heaven's sake. It was living with him in the same house that made her forget. Sitting across the dinner table, sharing the first pot of coffee each morning, undermined her professional detachment toward him, such as it was. She'd have to watch herself more carefully.

"Let's go. You've got a date, remember?"

She almost groaned. The last thing she wanted to do was get dressed up to attend a fund-raising banquet to reelect Alderman Rezlab.

"With that expression on your face, it should be a great evening for your Jason."

"He's not *my* Jason. He's my *friend* Jason. And I'll be fine. A shower and a change of clothes and I'll look forward to the evening," she claimed optimistically.

"That's the spirit," Aaron said.

She had been mistaken.

Thirty minutes later, she had showered but she still didn't look forward to the banquet. What was the matter with her? She had a chance to dress up and go somewhere other than a burned building or the office, something she hadn't done in ages. It would be a nice change. And she'd always enjoyed Jason's company in the past, so why couldn't she get excited about that now? Because she would rather stay home with Aaron, even if he spent the entire evening in his room on the off chance that he might come out, and she'd catch another glimpse of him? Good grief, was she that hung up on the man?

"Idiot," she told her reflection. "You're going to the banquet with Jason and you're going to have a nice time. Or *act* like you're having a nice time."

Her voice woke Vulcan who blinked at her once before drifting back to sleep on Karin's bed.

Resolutely she reached for the jar of foundation to camouflage her sunburned nose. She must have sweated off the sun block she'd applied that morning and no wonder. It had been hot enough to soften the repaired patches in the asphalt. The smell of hot tar made her think of the stench of burning buildings.

While Karin got ready for her date, her thoughts drifted to their arsonist. Two-Point came and went in and out of a four-block area, carrying something large enough in which to hide a two-gallon gasoline can, yet nobody noticed him. That was impossible. So why didn't anyone remember him? Because he was a man who lived there. Karin frowned. No. Two-Point was a pro and professional arsonists didn't live in the neighborhoods they torched. With the kind of fees a pro was paid, he could afford to live far from the rundown area he was burning down.

Whom else did people see and not pay any attention to? The postman. Delivery men. Utility repairmen. Meter readers. Garbage collectors. That was it! Karin grabbed her small evening bag and raced downstairs as fast as her high-heeled pumps permitted.

"Aaron, where are you?"

"In here," he called to her from the living room.

"I think I know why nobody remembers seeing Two-Point," she said, her voice excited and a little breathless from her mad dash down the stairs.

"Take it easy." Aaron couldn't help but take in every inch of her appearance. She looked great. Her skin, slightly tanned from her canvassing of neighborhoods, formed a pleasing contrast to her pale hair and blue-green eyes. Her generous mouth gleamed with some sort of pink lip gloss, making him ache to kiss it.

"Aaron, did you hear what I said?"

Catching his wayward thoughts, he said, "Yes. So tell me, why doesn't anybody remember him?"

"Because he poses as a repairman of some kind."

Aaron considered that. "Yes, that's possible. Even at night, trucks are out repairing telephone and other utility lines."

"It wouldn't be too hard to fix up a truck to look like one belonging to the telephone company, the water department, or the gas company."

"Not to mention cable television or the electric company. First thing tomorrow morning, I want you and Simon to go back to the same neighborhood and ask about utility trucks."

"Too bad we didn't think of this sooner. By now, the witnesses of the earlier fires won't remember if they saw utility trucks in the area on the night of the fires. Too much time has elapsed."

"Maybe, but if you get lucky tomorrow it'll be worth the time to question those witnesses. It'll be good corroborating evidence."

Karin nodded. She felt Aaron scrutinizing her appearance. "What's wrong? Is my slip showing?"

"You look lovely."

"Thank you." Karin glanced down at the scoop-necked, beige chiffon dress whose only ornament was a wide sash of the same material circling her waist. Did she look too blah?

Almost as if Aaron could read her thoughts, he said. "I once told you nothing you could ever wear, including grungy training fatigues, could make you look plain. You recall that?"

She remembered the incident vividly. She'd been a probationer at the fire station. Aaron had come to pick her up at the training field where her company had scaled walls and a roof in a simulated fire. She'd been sweaty, hot and tired, but one smile and his words had lifted her ten inches off the ground. The heated kisses that followed had rocketed her into seventh heaven. Would she ever feel such intense happiness again? Probably not. Despair knifed through her. Quickly, Karin crossed to the window and made a point of looking for Jason's car. Then she sat down and crossed her legs. It wasn't until she shifted her weight that she saw the snag in her nylon.

"Oh no! A snag! That'll turn into a run all the way down to my ankle before I even get to the banquet."

They heard the sound of a slammed car door.

"And Jason's here. Please, Aaron, can you let him in and tell him I'll be back down as soon as I change my hose?" Karin was already out in the hall when she heard Aaron promise to do as she'd asked.

When Karin came back into the living room, Jason sat stiffly on the edge of the couch. Aaron had positioned his wheelchair so that the two men faced each other. The room vibrated with tension. As soon as Jason saw Karin, he jumped up with alacrity. He greeted her with the smile of a man reprieved from the firing squad.

"Karin, we'd better go or we'll be late," Jason said. "Nice meeting you, Aaron." Without waiting for a reply, he took her elbow and turned her toward the door.

Karin found herself being hustled out with unseemly speed. On the way to Jason's car, she asked, "What's wrong?"

"Simon Legree back there," Jason said, inclining his head toward the house. "What's his problem?"

"What did Aaron say to you?"

"That I had to bring you back at a decent hour because you had a big day tomorrow, that you were on call twenty-four hours, that if your beeper went off in the middle of the banquet I had to drive you back here immediately. Stuff like that. The guy acts like he owns you."

"He does, in a way. I'm his personal assistant and I am on call round the clock."

Jason held the car door open for Karin. "I got the distinct impression that there was a lot more to it than that." After he slid behind the wheel, he asked, "Care to tell me about it?"

Karen sighed. "Remember when you got back from your six-months stint with the Springfield branch?" she asked.

"Yeah. You were just getting over some guy . . . Jeez, don't tell me that was Aaron?"

"It was."

"What a rotten break!"

"Tell me about it."

"You poor kid." Jason shook his head in sympathy. "Now, you not only work for the guy, but live in his house. How are you handling that?"

"How do you think? With a lot of anxiety and uncertainty," Karin said dryly. "Let's not talk about it now. I need a complete break tonight."

"All right." Jason started the car. "So far neither one of us has been particularly lucky in relationships, have we? But our luck is bound to change soon."

Was it? Karin didn't share Jason's optimism but he was right about their misfortunes and pain in affairs of the heart. Jason had been engaged to Karin's best friend and roommate in college. A month before the wedding Jenny had been diagnosed with a particularly virulent strain of leukemia. Three months later she had died. Mourning the lovely, gentle woman they'd both loved, cemented their friendship. Jason was the brother Karin never had.

Karin reached out to touch Jason's hand comforting-ly. "Well, we'd better get going, hadn't we? If I have to listen to a politician's promises, I don't want to do it on an empty stomach. I'm hungry."

Alderman Rezlab droned on and on. Karin didn't mind. The roast beef had been tender, the potatoes fluffy, the broccoli crisp. And the chocolate mousse alone had been worth getting dressed up for. With her face turned toward the microphone she appeared to be listening.

In reality she was daydreaming about a dark-haired, hazel-eyed man who'd said she looked lovely. Aaron had actually complimented her. She knew he'd been strongly attracted to her in the past. From what he'd said and from that gleam in his eyes, he was still attracted to her. The problem was, would Aaron ever do anything about this attraction as long as he was wheelchair-bound? All those long months ago, he'd convinced her that he never would.

Maybe living together had shown Aaron that being in a wheelchair made no difference to her. She had told him as much in the hospital but words hadn't convinced him. Maybe their actual day-to-day togetherness had. Hope surged through Karin like a bracing breath of fresh, cool air.

Don't hope, she told herself, tamping down the joyous feeling. She could be setting herself up for a painful fall. How often could she pick herself up and go on? One or two encouraging incidents hardly equaled a complete turnabout in Aaron's attitude. Still—

The applause around her signaled the conclusion of the speech and of Karin's happy daydream.

On the way home they talked of family and of mutual friends. All the while Karin had the impression Jason was playing for time. After he'd parked the car in front of Aaron's house, he finally broached the subject he'd skirted all evening. His voice was studiedly casual.

"I enjoyed going to the movie with Alice. We had a good time. Is she seeing anyone?"

Ah, at last, Karin thought, hiding her surprised joy. It was time Jason started to date again. He'd mourned his fiancée long and hard. Imitating his offhand manner, she said, "No, Alice isn't dating anyone special." From his expression, Karin could tell he was pleased by her answer. "She's taking this deadly boring class on tests and measurements. I'm sure she'd like to take in a movie or a concert with you."

"You think she really would?" he asked eagerly.

"Yes, I'm sure. Why don't you give her a call?"

"I will."

Jason escorted Karin to the front porch.

"You want to come in for a cup of coffee?" she asked.

Casting a quick look at the door, he said, "If you don't mind, I'll take a rain check."

They said good night. Karin had the impression that

Jason was anxious to get off that porch. She wondered if he had told her everything Aaron had said to him earlier.

The front door opened before Karin could insert her key in the lock.

"I heard you," Aaron said in explanation. "No sense in digging for your key."

Karin entered the house and closed the door behind her before she faced Aaron with a frown. "If I didn't know better, I'd swear you were lurking by the front door the way my mother used to do when I was out on dates in high school."

"But you know better, don't you," he remarked in a lofty manner, wheeling himself into the living room.

"I'm not sure that I do," Karin muttered, following him.

"Jason didn't want to come in for a nightcap?"

"No. Usually he does." Carefully, intently, she examined Aaron's face. There wasn't a trace of guilt on it. He looked as innocent as a baby. That in itself was suspicious. "Aaron, did you give Jason the third degree before I came down?"

"Of course, I didn't. What do you take me for? Karin, I'm surprised at you. I'd never presume to meddle like that in your private life."

His protest sounded sincere. At least on the surface it did, but there was something about Aaron's body language that made her think he was more than capable of meddling in her private life. She couldn't put her finger on it, but it was there nevertheless. Every ounce of her feminine intuition fueled that hunch.

"Why don't you sit down and finish watching the game with me? The Cubs are leading five to four in the seventh inning." Aaron pointed to the armchair next to him in an inviting gesture.

Karin accepted his invitation and it wasn't only because she liked baseball. Usually Aaron spent the evenings alone in his room, almost as if he wanted to hide from her. Intensely curious as to why he had broken the pattern, Karin sat in the chair he had indicated.

From time to time, she slanted searching glances in his direction, but his whole attention seemed focused on the ball game. Karin didn't mind. It gave her a chance to look at him. She loved doing that. She'd always loved looking at him. "Do your feet still hurt?" Aaron asked.

Karin hadn't noticed that she'd kicked off her pumps. "Yes. Wearing heels didn't help." She raised her feet. She arched and flexed them, but that didn't ease the discomfort.

"I know just the cure."

Without warning, Aaron lifted her left foot onto his thigh. Karin was too surprised to object. By the time she found her voice, his fingers were working magic on her aching foot. All she could do was sigh blissfully. His hands cradled her foot. His thumbs moved in circles over the sole, easing the burning sensation, releasing tension she hadn't even known she'd felt there. With a half-smile she leaned back in the chair and abandoned herself to the pleasure of his touch.

"I never knew a foot massage could feel this good," Karin said when he reached for her other foot. "You could make a fortune doing this."

"And give up the glamour of our job?" he asked, his voice filled with mock consternation.

"No more digging through rubble," Karin added.

"No more sifting ashes for hours on end searching for clues."

"No more sniffing sodden beams for the telltale odor of an accelerant." Karin wrinkled her nose.

"No more chasing down greedy people who took the easy way out by torching their property."

"No more filling out endless forms and reports."

"Give up all that? Nah." Aaron dragged out the "nah" as if it contained a dozen vowels instead of one.

They smiled at each other in perfect understanding. Where their profession was concerned they were on the same page, Karin reflected. If only . . . no, she couldn't, wouldn't, think in personal terms.

"Speaking of our profession, your mother called."

"Oh, yeah? But how did you get from our profession to my mother?" Karin asked, intrigued.

"She called about the ladies auxiliary. Seems it's time once again for their annual fund-raiser. You know, chicken and rice followed by an auction of everyone's white elephants. I said we'd come."

Karin groaned. "How could you?"

"Now, now. It's for a good cause. The proceeds go for scholarships for orphans of firefighters. You can choke down the overcooked chicken and the underdone rice. And the desserts are excellent. The ladies bring homemade pies. We're going early because I want to stake out a piece of Mrs. Schneider's peach pie. It's fit for the gods."

"Why did you say I'd go? That was more than a little high-handed of you."

"No, it wasn't. I did it mostly to keep you off the black list the battalion chief keeps of those who play hooky from this affair. It's his favorite charity. Probably because he was one of the orphans who received help years ago."

Karin threw him a doubting look. "What do you mean, 'mostly'?"

"You don't want either of us to show up without an escort, do you? That would set a dozen wives to matchmaking with the result that neither of us would be able to concentrate on our work the way we do now."

"And what do you think will happen when you show up with me? You think that won't set tongues wagging? Maybe I should wear a sign saying that I'm your assistant, not your date."

Ignoring her ironic tone, he said, "That wouldn't work. Everyone would think you protested too much and suspect that something *was* going on between us.

Besides, it wouldn't be strictly true that you'd be there as my assistant."

Karin looked at him expectantly, waiting for him to clarify his statement. He kept massaging her feet, both of which were now resting on his thigh. His fingers stroked her instep, turning her insides warm and weak. She felt like purring the way Vulcan did when she petted him.

The temptation to close her eyes and simply surrender to the pleasure of Aaron's touch was immense. Gripping the arms of the chair, she fought against the seductive languor that seeped all the way to her bones. She couldn't afford to be that relaxed, that off guard. In this state, heaven only knew what she might say or do. "Explain that 'strictly true' bit," she finally managed to utter in a low tone.

"I can't order my assistant to go with me, and I can't ask you for a date because I'm your boss, so it has to be something in between. Do you follow me?"

She nodded. If she wasn't vigilant, she could be tempted to follow him to purgatory and back.

"Good. We'll eat together, and afterwards I'll bid on the treasure of your choice. A cuckoo clock, pruning shears, and a matched set of jelly glasses were last year's hottest items. This year we may even have a chance at a black velvet, paint-by-numbers portrait of Elvis."

Karin had to laugh in spite of herself. "I can hardly wait," she murmured.

"It won't be so bad. You'll see," he murmured.

When had his voice assumed that low, liquid, sexy tone? When had his fingers stopped massaging and started caressing? Or was she merely imagining the different touch? His thumbs stroked the length of her feet lightly, gently. That was definitely not a move listed in any massage manual. And when had the skirt of her dress slid up, revealing a good deal of her thighs? Quickly, Karin sat up, pulled her feet out of Aaron's hands, and smoothed her skirt down.

"Sure you don't want me to rub your feet some more?"

"Quite sure. Thanks."

Just then Sosa hit a home run with the bases loaded.

"Yes," Aaron yelled, pumping his arm in that typical male gesture of victory. With a huge grin he watched the men round the bases to score. "Well, that's that. We won." He clicked off the television. Turning to Karin, he asked, "So, how was your da . . . banquet?"

"Okay."

"Just okay?"

"Yes."

"Part of that might have been my fault."

"Oh? So you did interrogate Jason."

"I wouldn't call it that. We talked about the demands of your job and I pointed out the necessity of you getting enough sleep, among other things."

"Thanks. You're worse than my mother ever dreamed of being."

"He didn't kiss you good night, did he?" Aaron asked.

He sounded pleased by that, Karin thought. "No, Jason didn't kiss me. Not that it's any of your business. I told you, we're only friends."

"I owe you a good night kiss then."

Thinking she must have misunderstood him, Karin turned her head. He was leaning toward her, his face only inches from hers. Her gaze widened in surprise. Karin stared into his intense hazel eyes until they were so close they became the whole universe. Overwhelmed, she let her eyelids flutter shut.

Karin felt herself sway until Aaron's strong hands framed her face. Their heat seared her skin. A small shiver zigzagged down her spine. She knew if she allowed Aaron to kiss her, she would be lost. Yet even knowing this, she was helpless to keep her lips from parting for him in welcome.

Aaron wasn't a man who ever did anything in a tentative manner, but when he first brushed his lips against Karin's, the touch was careful, restrained, as if he clung to the illusion that this could be one of those nice, civilized good night kisses couples exchanged on their first date.

It wasn't.

Their emotions ignited like a lighted match tossed into a pile of accelerant-soaked newspapers. Aaron kissed her deeply, hungrily, repeatedly. His touch burned her. His mouth inflamed her senses. Her blood thrummed heavily through her veins and pounded in her temples until she thought she would lose all capacity for rational thought. Her fingers dug into his shoulders in a desperate effort to retain at least a tenuous hold on reality.

When he ended the kiss Aaron pressed his face into her hair. Karin felt his breath warmly against her ear.

"Good night, Karin," he whispered, his voice tight and raspy.

Pressing her hands against her hot face, she watched him roll away. Every cell in her body screamed for her to stop him, to call him back, to rush after him. Drawing on every last ounce of strength and self-control, she remained seated in dazed silence. It wasn't until Aaron had disappeared through the door that Karin realized she had bitten the inside of her cheek until she tasted blood. Exhausted by the intense emotions of the past minutes, she allowed herself to slump in the chair like a rag doll.

She had been right in letting him go. They needed time to come to terms with that kiss. Now what, she wondered, her heart pounding with anxiety. Where would they go from here? They still had to work together. How would they treat each other after that explosive kiss? Pretend it hadn't happened? Resolve it wouldn't happen again? Decide that for the good of the department she would have to leave? She sighed deeply. None of these possibilities was exactly something to look forward to.

Karin's head throbbed painfully. There was nothing she could do tonight. She might as well go to bed. Not that she expected to do much except toss and turn for hours. And pray.

Chapter Eight

At two in the morning the telephone rang.

Aaron picked up the receiver a second after Karin did. The dispatcher informed them of a warehouse fire across the tracks from the Knoll Brothers Furniture Store. Since this fire had been spotted in its early stages and they had a chance of observing its progress, Karin was acutely aware of the necessity of getting there as soon as possible. She managed to back the van out of the alley seven minutes after the call.

"Step on it," Aaron said.

That was only the second sentence he'd spoken since the phone had rung, the first being a terse command to hurry as she'd come running down the steps. After tossing and turning for several hours wondering what he would say when they met after that explosive, unex-

pected kiss, his matter-of-fact utterances were definitely anticlimactic. She swung the magnetic bubble light
on top of the van.

Since there was little traffic, Karin could take her
eyes off the road from time to time to glance in the
rearview mirror. His expression somber, Aaron
watched the neon-lit urban landscape flashing by. She
suspected that he didn't actually see any of the scenery,
that his thoughts were focused on something else. Their
kiss? Intuitively she guessed that the more time passed
without them discussing it, the better it would be.
Perhaps they could keep things the way they had been
after all.

Did she want that? She'd thought of little else all
night and had come to no conclusion. All she knew was
that she'd loved being kissed by Aaron and kissing him
back. And yes, she did want him to kiss her again. She
also wanted to keep on working with him, living with
him. Was that possible?

Glancing at Aaron, she tried to gauge his mood.
Somber. Introspective. Troubled. She knew him well
enough to realize he had to regret kissing her. He'd broken the rules he'd set up for himself in the hospital.
He'd fallen short of his own expectations and for a man
like him, that was nothing to be proud of. Time would
lessen his regret and recriminations. Time might even
tempt him to kiss her again. Time was decidedly her
ally. Encouragement coursed through her.

Careful not to let Aaron catch her looking at him, she

kept her glances brief, though she longed to gaze at his face long and intently. He hadn't had time to shave. His cheeks and chin were covered with the night's growth of beard. She wondered if the rough stubble against her sensitive skin would add a new dimension to the sensuous joy she would feel. Imagining it, her skin tingled. Heat flooded her body.

Karin popped the second and third snap of her cotton shirt for relief.

Aaron caught the movement. He felt suffocatingly hot himself. He hadn't bothered to put on a tie since it was one of those oppressively muggy Midwestern summer nights that would take the starch out of a Boston banker in thirty seconds flat.

He watched Karin's fingers push a wisp of her fair hair under the thick twist on top of her head. Earlier that evening she'd worn it in an elegant coil, so she must have taken it down when she'd gone to sleep. Lying in his narrow bed night after night, he'd pictured that silvery mane spread over his pillow upstairs while she slept in his bed.

Karin's hair had felt like liquid silk in his eager hands. It was as pleasurable to touch as her face. He could still feel the fine, firm texture of her skin under his fingertips, the contours of her high cheekbones, and the beguiling softness of her lips. The memory of her mouth pressed against his, opening just enough to invite him to explore its sweet depth, almost caused him to groan out loud. He'd thought he would drown in that kiss. He'd wanted it to go on forever.

He'd also known he should have pulled back the instant his mouth had caressed hers. Blast, he'd known he shouldn't have kissed her in the first place. He'd known he shouldn't have touched her even as his hands had reached out to capture the face that haunted his every unguarded moment. He'd known from that shattering second he'd wakened in the hospital and hadn't been able to move his legs that he had to renounce Karin. She deserved a man who was whole in every respect.

Knowing all that, why in heaven's name hadn't he stopped himself? Aaron had spent the sleepless hours until the telephone rang torturing himself with that unanswerable question.

Nothing had changed since the day he'd sent her away. He was still a prisoner in a wheelchair. He was still damaged goods. He was still a cripple.

Cripple.

The word tore at him, evoking echoes from the past, a voice spitting out the word like an obscenity. He had been too young to know its meaning, but there had been no doubt in his mind that it was something he must never turn into, or he, too, would be sent away, rejected like damaged goods. Sweat beaded on Aaron's forehead. He wiped it off. If only he could wipe out the memories of the past as easily. But he couldn't. What he could do, was put them aside and concentrate on the problems of the present.

The biggest problem was Karin. What on earth was he going to do about her? More to the point, what was he going to do about his feelings for her? At first he'd thought that he had torn them out of his heart. Then he'd thought he'd be strong enough to prevent himself from experiencing them again. When he'd realized he couldn't do that, he'd thought he'd be tough enough not to act on them. Obviously he'd been wrong. As wrong as a man could be.

Aaron was honest enough to admit that what had driven him to act was pure jealousy. He couldn't endure watching Karin go off with another man. Every male instinct imprinted on his genes had reared up in protest. Every age-old masculine trait had demanded that he fight for his woman. Every noble intention, every lofty vow to leave her alone had disintegrated in the face of his fundamental attraction to her.

Blast and triple blast.

None of this had been part of his plan. He'd honestly thought that he could work with Karin without succumbing to her all over again. Had he fueled his attraction by asking her to move in with him? Not really. All that had done was speed up the process. Aaron now realized that it had been inevitable. He had deep feelings for Karin. There was nothing he could do about them. Even though he could not root out his feelings for her, he didn't have to give in to them again. He didn't have to act on them. He mustn't, he *couldn't*, act on them.

What if he never walked again? Usually he banished this thought into the deepest recesses of his mind, but for once he couldn't do so. Karin had sworn that the wheelchair didn't change how she felt about him. Could that be possible? He brooded about it, but didn't allow himself to believe it.

He would double his therapy sessions. That would be exhausting and excruciatingly painful. He balled his hands into fists. Still, it was easier to endure the physical pain than the emotional pain of wanting this woman in vain. Each agonizing session would bring him closer to the day he could walk again. Karin's voice roused him from his brooding thoughts.

"From the number of sirens it sounds like another big one," she said.

Aaron was grateful she had interrupted his thoughts. It was time to focus on the job, not indulge in unrealistic, torturous dreams. "It's probably Two-Point again. Confound him. I'd hoped we'd catch him before he torched another building."

"If we can start the stakeouts soon, we're bound to nab him. I can't wait."

"Me either. He's getting entirely too brazen."

As soon as they arrived on the fire scene, both knew it was Two-Point's job. The blaze was working its way to the middle of the warehouse, indicating that it had started at both ends. Without wasting words, they set out to do their usual tasks. Karin shot two rolls of film. She walked around the perimeter of the fire, studying the people who'd gathered to watch. Aaron had stationed himself at the command post. He consulted with the man in charge, offered helpful suggestions, and fielded questions with his cell phone.

Hours later when the blaze was extinguished and the fire scene secured, they compared notes.

"Did you find anything unusual?" Aaron asked her.

"No. Except that the owners who live nearby heard the sirens and came to see what was going on."

"Oh?"

"It's not what you think. I'm sure they're not pyromaniacs who came to get their kicks by watching the fire."

"You're sure?"

"Absolutely. They were completely distraught, which made their English even more difficult to understand, but from what I could make out, all their stock was in that warehouse which seems to be a total loss. They own a Vietnamese grocery store four blocks north of here. I've got the address."

"Since you made contact with them I want you to interview them first thing in the morning. I'll get Simon and Bryan to take samples from the arson site."

"Okay."

"We may as well head home for a couple of hours of sleep."

Head home. *What lovely words*, Karin thought. They

shared a lot of things in the house on Kenmore Street. Now that she knew Aaron still cared about her, she felt encouraged. If she held on long enough, there just might be a chance for them to work out their problems. Her heart filled with cautious joy.

When Aaron joined her in the kitchen the next morning, Karin was setting up the ironing board.

"Breakfast's ready," she said, "such as it is. Whole grain bagels, cream cheese and cantaloupe."

"Sounds good to me." Aaron poured himself a cup of coffee.

"You're easy to please. That sort of surprises me," Karin admitted.

"Why?" Aaron looked at her, waiting for an answer with undisguised interest.

"Because you're so demanding at work. And you were a dyed-in-the wool tyrant at the academy."

With deceptive calm he asked, "Consequently you reasoned that my demanding ways would carry over into my private life?"

Feeling defensive, she said, "You have to admit that this isn't an entirely illogical assumption."

"No, except even dyed-in-the-wool tyrants have their softer sides. Besides, I hate to cook, so I'm grateful every time someone else does it. Maybe I haven't told you how much I appreciate everything you do around here. Thanks, Karin."

She could feel the pleasant warmth aroused by his

thanks flush her face with color. "You don't have to thank me. It's as easy to cook for two as it is for one."

"Sort of like two can live as cheaply as one?"

Karin responded to the amused twinkle in his hazel eyes with a smile. "That, I think, is a fallacy that people used when they felt they had to justify getting married."

"You don't think getting married needs justification?"

"No."

"Then why haven't you ever married?"

"Now you sound like my mother. Give me a break! I'm only twenty-five. That's hardly knocking at the gates of perpetual spinsterhood."

"And?" he prompted, undeterred by her flip answer.

"And I haven't met the man I wanted as a husband." What a lie. The man, the only man, she wanted, had ever wanted, was sitting only four feet away. Afraid that her face might betray her, Karin's mind searched frantically for a pretext to turn away. The iron. Bending over it, she pretended to check its temperature setting. Her long hair, which she hadn't pinned up in its usual twist yet, fell like a curtain around her face, concealing her expression.

Aaron was the only man she'd ever dreamed of marrying. If she couldn't have him, she didn't want anyone else. At least not for a long, long time. Karin didn't know how she knew this with such absolute certainty, only that she did. She would live alone. If necessary, she would take care of her mother in her old age. She would be Aunt Karin to her sisters' children and spoil them with extravagant birthday presents. She would take in stray animals and give them a good home. That's what her life would be like unless Aaron Knight recovered the use of his legs and asked her to be his wife.

She was really going off the deep end, dreaming of marriage when she didn't know for sure how Aaron felt about her. He'd only kissed her once recently. All that sizzling kiss had told her was that he'd desired her at that moment. Nothing more. To build marriage dreams on that was unrealistic beyond belief. She wasn't a woman who ordinarily indulged in flights of fancy, and this was no time to start. She reached for the can of spray starch and shook it vigorously.

Aaron watched her. Intrigued he asked, "What are you doing?"

"Putting some starch in this cotton jumpsuit. According to the weatherman, the city will be an oven today. Without starch, the outfit will be limp and wrinkled before I get to my first interview." If only she could spray some starch on her imagination to keep it from running wild. "You want your investigators to look neat, don't you?"

"You always look neat, even in the middle of the night when you have five minutes to get ready," Aaron said. He took a sip of coffee. "You're seeing the Vietnamese family, right? Should I try to locate an interpreter?"

"No. Not yet. Their son speaks English. At least that's what I think the woman said last night."

After she finished ironing, Karin went upstairs to dress. Since the natural-colored cotton outfit was plain, she added a woven, multi-hued belt. With her hair coiled and simple silver hoop earrings, she thought she looked neat, cool, and professional.

On the way to the office they discussed the latest fire. Aaron still hadn't mentioned their kiss. That was encouraging. Very encouraging. At least Karin interpreted it as a sign that he wasn't brooding about it and regretting it. If he didn't regret the kiss, he might just repeat it. And if he was able to kiss her, he might be able to forgive her for the argument on that fateful day. In time they might reach that emotional intimacy she craved. The thought sent more hope rushing to her heart.

At the office, she watched him propel the wheelchair up the ramp before she nosed the van back into traffic.

She found the grocery store in the heart of a three-block area that seemed to be solidly Southeast Asian. This didn't surprise her. It followed the pattern of all new groups of immigrants. A little over a century ago, her ancestors had settled in the northern part of Chicago, turning a sizable area into Little Sweden.

At the store, a boy who looked to be about nine, acted as interpreter. Karin asked the usual questions about insurance, about having enemies, about having received threats. All the answers were negative. Thinking of the mysterious real estate agent who'd wanted to acquire the Knoll Brothers Furniture Store, Karin asked, "Has anyone tried to buy the warehouse from your parents?" The boy translated her question and his parents' answer.

"The warehouse belongs to Mr. Crawford. My family rents it from him."

The woman who'd spoken to Karin last night said something else to him.

"My mom says Mr. Crawford wanted us to get out of the warehouse."

"Did he say why?"

"No."

"Did your parents agree to get out?"

"No. They say we've got a lease for a whole year. A lawyer wrote it up and he said it was legal."

"Do you have Mr. Crawford's address?"

After an animated exchange, Mr. Crawford's address and phone number were produced. Karin copied them. She spent a few more minutes asking questions, but it was obvious that the family knew nothing about the fire. Nor had anyone noticed a dark-colored van near the warehouse. That wasn't unusual, since it was several blocks from the store.

Karin drove back to the fire site. She interviewed all the residents in the adjacent block. By noon the sun was so hot and bright, the air shimmered crystalline. She called the office only to learn that Aaron had left for a physical therapy session with his cousin.

"He always goes in the evenings. Is something

wrong?" Karin asked Molly, anxiety constricting her lungs.

"It's odd him going on his lunch hour," Molly conceded, "but he seemed okay to me. Maybe his therapist couldn't take him this evening."

"That's probably it," Karin said, only too glad to find a reasonable explanation. Aaron *had* looked fine that morning, she reminded herself. Reassured, she located a restaurant where she cooled off with two glasses of iced coffee and ate a Greek salad before she continued her interviews.

At 5:00 she dragged herself into the office.

Molly, who was tidying her desk, looked at Karin and said, "Heavens, girl, you look all done in."

"I feel as wilted as a wet dishrag." Glancing at her clothes, she said, "I *look* like a wet rag. You'd never know I starched and ironed this jumpsuit this morning."

"I made some iced tea. Why don't you get yourself a glass?"

"Thanks, I will."

"Oh, and your mother called. Nothing's wrong, but she wants you to call her back as soon as possible. She'll be at her store until six."

"Thanks." Karin poured herself a tumbler of tea and downed it on the spot. She refilled the glass and carried it to her desk where she dialed the number of the floral shop.

"Hi, Mom. What's up?"

"Just calling to find out what you're going to wear to the auction dinner."

Karin groaned. "Mom, I haven't given that any thought yet." She heard her mother's weary sigh. "Mom, we've been really busy."

"That's what I was afraid of, and that's why I called to remind you. Have you bought yourself any new dresses lately?"

"No. I haven't had time to go shopping. Besides, I wear dresses so rarely that I don't really need any new ones."

"Wrong, darling. You'll need a new one for the dinner."

"Why? I've got several in my closet to choose from."

Hedwig Bergstrom made a most unladylike harumping noise. "Darling girl, the dresses in your closet only a little old lady might wear. Correction. *I'm* almost a little old lady and I wouldn't be caught dead in one of your dresses."

Stung, Karin said, "There's nothing wrong with them. They're good quality clothes. I paid a lot for them."

"I know you buy good quality clothes. I taught you that, remember? It's just that your clothes lack . . . oomph. They're so understated that they border on being boring. You know, when your sisters were teenagers, I always had to tell them to tone down their makeup and their clothes. You, on the other hand, always looked like you were ready to disappear into the wallpaper."

"I'm too big to disappear into the wallpaper."

"You're not too big. You're statuesque. And beautiful. Like those figures the Vikings carved into the prows of their ships."

"That's nice of you to say, Mom, but—"

"Why don't you invite Alice to help you pick out a new dress? Something bright and young. She's got great taste in clothes. Want me to call her and set it up?"

Karin sighed. She might as well capitulate right then and there. Her mother was quite capable of going out to buy her a dress if she didn't do it herself.

"Mom, I promise I'll go shopping for a dress."

"Nothing in beige, gray or navy."

"Okay, okay."

"Pick something in a warm, bright color. Something young."

"Yes, Mom."

"You'll never know who might be at the auction. We might even draw a few eligible bachelors."

"Mom, don't start with the matchmaking. And don't fix me up with anybody," Karin pleaded.

"Would I do that?"

"Yes, you would, and you have."

As soon as she hung up, Karin wondered when she could fulfill her promise of buying a new dress. If Aaron had succeeded in setting up the stake outs, she wouldn't have time to go shopping. Her mother would be upset if she showed up in one of her old dresses. Karin shrugged. She couldn't help that. Catching an arsonist was just slightly more important than a new dress.

After rereading her notes, Karin tried Crawford's number for the fifth time. He wasn't in. Where was that man? She needed to talk to him. In frustration, she swore softly. It had been another wasted day. Except for a glimmer of an idea that had nagged at her all day. She went to the conference room. Standing in front of the large, hand-drawn map of Two-Point's fires, the cold glass of tea pressed against her forehead, she studied the squares representing houses and empty lots. After a while she reached for a box of colored pencils and began shading in the squares.

"Are you just practicing staying within the lines or is there a purpose to your coloring?" Aaron asked.

Karin grinned. "I'll have you know I was the best staying-inside-the-lines colorer in my kindergarten class. My mother still has the certificate that says so."

"Yeah? I bet you were cute as a button to boot."

So were you, I bet. Karin could envision Aaron as a little boy, all dark curls and mischievous eyes. If they were to have a little boy, would he—quickly, Karin dismissed the thought. *Quit daydreaming!* Concentrate on the job. Listening to the whoosh of the wheels, she waited until Aaron stopped his chair beside her before she spoke again.

"I had another one of those days where I only eliminated possibilities. Didn't come across a single clue or lead, so I kept thinking about the motive. A good professional torch like Two-Point isn't hired to burn anything randomly. He's undoubtedly too expensive for anyone to employ to torch houses on a whim. There's got to be a reason why these particular properties are being burned down."

Aaron grunted in agreement.

"There's got to be a pattern. I kept visualizing that area. That wasn't hard. I feel like it's burned into my brain," she added. "And I think I've found a pattern."

"Oh? Show me."

Pointing to the map, she said, "The red squares are Two-Point's arson sites. The yellow are empty lots. The orange are houses that have been condemned or abandoned due to disrepair, former fires, water damage or whatever. The few green squares are buildings still in use."

Karin paused to study Aaron's face. From his animated expression she could tell he saw what she had seen.

"If he takes out those few remaining buildings, somebody's got four city blocks of urban property waiting to be developed," he said.

"Exactly."

Karin studied the map some more. Then the flaw in her reasoning hit her. "But it's all wrong," she said, her voice defeated. She collapsed sideways onto the hard chair, laying her arms across its back before resting her cheek on them. "The warehouse fire throws a monkey wrench into the pattern. It's west of the railroad. Who's going to build something with railroad tracks running through it?"

"A lot of people. You're thinking of passenger service. Think freight."

Karin transferred her attention from the map to Aaron. "Freight? I'm sorry, but I don't see what you're getting at."

"Shipping freight by rail has always been economical. Suppose the area is slated for industrial development. Access to rails would be a plus."

Aaron reached out to squeeze Karin's hand encouragingly. His touch, more than his words, infused her with strength and new enthusiasm. She straightened up. "That would make sense. Now all we have to find out is who's buying up all the land. And I have a lead." Karin told him about Crawford who owned the torched warehouse.

"Good job! Keep trying to reach him," Aaron said. "But now let's go home."

"It's barely six o'clock!"

"Bergstrom, are you complaining that I'm letting you go at the normal quitting time?"

"Just surprised," she said hastily.

"I'm going to work on the stake out schedule at home before I go to therapy."

Alarm shot through Karin. Clutching the hand he'd laid across hers, she demanded, "What's wrong? You've already been to therapy today."

"Nothing's wrong. As a matter of fact, the session at noon went so well that my therapist is going to start me on a new routine tonight."

Karin's knees went rubbery with relief. Her voice sounded tremulous when she whispered, "That's wonderful."

"Yeah, it's encouraging."

Though Aaron was downplaying this news, Karin could tell he was deeply pleased and hopeful. Karen said a silent, quick prayer.

"Don's picking me up at eight."

Only now the significance of that sank in and galvanized Karin into action. "You've got to eat at least an hour before therapy. We better hurry home right now."

Aaron squeezed her hand before he released it. "We'll make it."

They *would* make it, Karin vowed. And she wasn't just thinking of that evening's schedule.

"Yes, we'll make it." She flashed Aaron a happy, confident smile.

Chapter Nine

Karen parked her car illegally. She justified this by telling herself that she would be in the loading zone only for thirty minutes at most. After displaying her special arson investigation card on the dashboard, she headed for Crawford's condominium.

The building was fancy enough to employ a doorman wearing a gray uniform with gold buttons. He eyed her warily as she approached. When she presented her ID, he assumed that air of bravado characteristic of people who'd run afoul of the law.

"I've been telephoning Mr. Crawford since noon yesterday without success. How can I reach him?"

"He's out of town."

"I assumed that. Where is he? When will he be back?"

"I don't know." The doorman shrugged indifferently, avoiding eye contact.

He was lying. When she spoke again, Karin's voice reflected her annoyance and her determination to get the truth out of him.

"Don't play games with me. You can answer my questions here or you can answer them in my office. I have the authority to bring you in."

The doorman shifted his weight.

"People who can afford to live in a building with a doorman usually tell him at least how long they'll be gone so he can keep an eye on their place. Usually they'll leave a number where they can be reached. Now, having had a chance to think about my question, please answer it."

The doorman's expression was resentful when he decided to cooperate. "Mr. Crawford is supposed to come back this afternoon. He went up to Door County for a short vacation."

"When did he leave?"

"Tuesday."

That figured. He'd given himself an alibi for the time of the warehouse fire on Wednesday evening.

"What did he do?" the doorman asked.

"I didn't say he did anything. A warehouse he owns burned to the ground."

"Oh yeah? What a shame."

"Thanks for your time."

"Shall I tell him you were here?"

Karin saw no reason to ask the doorman to keep her visit a secret. If she asked him and he talked anyway, Crawford might suspect that they were on to him. She wanted to face him when he was relatively off guard.

"You can tell him I was here and that I'll be back to get some information about the warehouse."

When Karin got back to her car she sat quietly for a few minutes, contemplating her next move. Not that she lacked for work and could afford to be idle. A small mountain of forms waited on her desk. Sooner or later she would have to fill them out. Since they wouldn't help them catch Two-Point, she decided to deal with them later. First, she wanted to take another look at his targeted neighborhood.

Karin wasn't sure what she hoped to find. Yet something compelled her to revisit the scene of Two-Point's arsons. Looked at objectively, the area had to be one of Chicago's least beautiful. Razing it and rebuilding from the ground up wasn't a bad idea. Doing it through arson was, though. With fire, not even the best arsonist could guarantee that nobody got hurt or killed. So far Two-Point had been lucky.

Driving slowly through the area, Karin tried to pick out which of the remaining buildings would be Two-Point's next target. It would help if she knew which hadn't been sold recently. Why hadn't she thought of that before? If their theory that someone was buying up the properties was correct, then one of the unsold buildings would be the arsonist's next victim.

After canvassing the block, Karin learned two things: which of the buildings had been sold recently and that they had been bought by a real estate conglomerate named something that sounded like Sunny or Son.

She also ran into Simon and Bryan who would undoubtedly tell Aaron of her solo trip to the arson area. Karin felt her trip had been necessary and justified.

An hour later she drove to the cafeteria near head-quarters to meet Alice for lunch. When they'd gone through the serving line and were comfortably seated, Karin said, "Okay, what do you want to talk about? The way you practically ordered me to meet you, makes me think you had an ulterior motive."

Alice grinned. "Your mother phoned."

Karin shook her head, her expression a mixture of resignation and annoyance. "Now why doesn't that surprise me? The woman never gives up. Okay, so what are you supposed to persuade me to do?"

"Take you shopping for a new dress."

Karin took a bread stick from the basket and snapped it in half. "That's what I suspected, but you're too late."

"Meaning you already bought a dress?"

"Yes. Why do you sound so surprised?" Karin demanded.

"Because in all the time we've lived together you never once accepted my invitation to go shopping. And it wasn't because you didn't have time. Admit it, Karin. You hate going shopping for clothes."

"It's not much fun for me. Because I'm so tall, I can't

just take any dress off the rack and wear it the way you can. Any size ten—"

"Size twelve," Alice corrected, with a sigh. Quickly, guiltily, she put down the dinner roll she'd just buttered.

". . . any size twelve fits you. Except for certain brand names, most dresses I find need alteration. That's why I like separates. More of them come in 'talls'."

"But you did find a new dress?"

Karin nodded. "I got lucky."

"When did you go shopping?"

"Last night. Since we're starting our stakeouts tonight, it was the only time I had to go before the dinner. I phoned you to invite you to go with me but you were out. It was sort of a spur-of-the-moment decision."

"What sort of dress did you buy?"

"It's not boring like my other dresses. 'Boring' is how my mother described them," Karin explained.

"Your mother's right. The neutrals you're partial to aren't all that exciting. What color is this dress?"

"Red."

Alice's fork stopped midway to her mouth. "You bought something in red?"

"Yes."

"You mean the dress is a dark shade of burgundy or maroon, don't you?"

"No. It's red. Fire-engine red."

"Well, I'll be." When Alice recovered from her surprise, she said, "Finally! I've been tempted to throw out your wardrobe and claim we've had a burglary." Alice paused to take a sip of water. "Red, huh? Fantastic. You're the kind of blond who can wear red. It's a great color for you." She paused to study her cousin. "What brought on this change? What did Aaron do to make you want to wear a red dress?"

"He kissed me."

"Judging by that blissful expression on your face, you want him to kiss you again, right?"

"Right."

"But?" Alice prompted when she saw Karin's smile fade.

"But he's fighting his attraction to me with every ounce of his formidable willpower and discipline. And maybe he's right. Maybe that's what I should continue to do, too. We're still working together, and he's still in that wheelchair." Karin sighed deeply.

"He still feels the way he did in the hospital?"

"I think so. Maybe the dress was a mistake. Maybe I should take it back."

"Describe the dress."

"It's got a round neckline. Sort of low but not overly provocative. Narrow straps over the shoulders and a narrow belt with a small rhinestone buckle. The full skirt stops just above the knees. And the material sort of shimmers and whispers when I move."

"Perfect. Sexy and dressy without being cheap and obvious. Did you buy hose to go with the dress?"

Karin's smile faltered. "No. I was so excited about the dress I forgot."

"Don't fret. I'll buy a pair for you. I know just the right kind to get."

"Not red, please."

"No, no. That would be overkill. Wear your off-white pumps. The hose I'm thinking of are silky and gossamer sheer. They'll show off your legs beautifully."

"You don't think I should take the dress back?"

"No. It sounds perfect for the party."

"Well, maybe it's time for me to stop wearing dresses not even a little old lady would wear."

"High time," Alice agreed with wholehearted enthusiasm.

That settled, Karin asked, "Where were you last night?"

"I had a date."

"Oh? A new man?"

"Sort of."

Karin waited.

"Actually, you know him. Jason took me to a movie."

Karin smiled. "He didn't waste any time."

"He said he talked to you about asking me out. Karin, are you sure you don't mind?"

"Don't you start on me, too. Jason and I are only friends. I'm delighted that he asked you for a date."

"Good. We're going to a concert at Grant Park on Saturday."

Alice spent the rest of the meal talking about Jason.

No sooner had Karin entered the reception area when Aaron spotted her. "In here, Bergstrom. Now."

"What's wrong?" Karin whispered to Molly as she passed the secretary.

"Beats me. He just got back from therapy."

Had Aaron suffered a setback in his recovery, Karin wondered, anxiety gripping her.

"Close the door and sit down."

"I'd just as soon stand—but, okay," she said, seeing his stormy expression.

"What's this I hear about you going on interviews alone?"

"Is that what's got you in such an uproar?" she asked, relieved.

"You bet it's got me in an uproar!" Aaron wheeled his chair from behind the desk to face her. Drilling her with angry eyes, he said, "Have you lost the sense God gave you? A woman walking alone through that neighborhood is asking for trouble."

"I went to the grocery store owners by myself and you didn't object."

"It's one thing to go alone to a specific place for an interview, but quite something else to canvass a whole neighborhood by yourself. All the other times you've been out you were with Simon, right?"

Karin didn't say anything. Apparently she didn't have to. Her expression revealed the truth, judging by the horror-stricken look on Aaron's face.

"Good God! I can't believe you were going house to house alone! That neighborhood is victimized by criminals of all sorts, by gangs, by guys strung out on heaven only knows what! Karin, I can't let myself think what might have happened to you." Aaron grabbed her shoulders and squeezed. "Promise you won't do it again."

Karin was ready to argue fiercely with him about being overprotective until she recognized the expression in his eyes. He was afraid for her. This realization knocked the props out from under her. She felt the warmth of his hands on her shoulders, a warmth that spread all the way to her fingertips.

"Karin?"

"I'm sorry. I really misunderstood your instructions," she managed to say.

"Promise you won't do it again. Humor me, Karin, please, and swear you won't go there alone anymore."

"Well, if you put it that way, I promise. Though it seems overly cautious to me. It's not as if I were some petite, puny, helpless girl. I'm a tall, strong woman, or haven't you noticed?"

"I've noticed. And I like what I've noticed. I like it a lot more than I should."

Karin savored his words. The anger in Aaron's eyes had turned to warmth. They were the most beautiful eyes she'd ever seen, eyes she wanted to gaze into forever. Except they heated her blood instantaneously, unstoppable, dangerously. For the first time, Karin understood what it mean to be on fire for someone. Aaron's thumbs moved back and forth, caressing her collar bone. Wanting, needing to touch him, her fingers curled around his upper arms.

Aaron groaned. "You could tempt a saint without half trying."

Then why not give in to temptation? she prompted silently.

His hands tightened on her shoulders. For a second she thought Aaron was going to pull her toward him. Then the muscles in his arms grew even more rocklike as he held her at arm's length.

"Karin, I'm a cripple."

"I don't think so."

"Are you blind, woman?"

"Maybe. And maybe I see more clearly and more deeply than you. I can see beyond your physical disability. It doesn't bother me."

"Well, it does me."

"I'm sure being in that chair is inconvenient, and the pain is obviously overwhelming at times, but it doesn't make you ugly or an outcast, not the way you seem to think it does. You say the word 'cripple' as if it were synonymous with 'leper' or 'untouchable'. Why do you think that?"

"It's a long and ugly story."

"Please tell me."

The intercom buzzed.

Karin cursed it silently but forcefully.

"Maybe we'll talk about it some other time," Aaron said as he wheeled himself back behind his desk.

"I'll hold you to that. I'll be in the squad room if you need me."

Karin sat at her desk, staring at the far wall. What long story did Aaron have to tell? It wasn't until then that it occurred to her she knew very little about his family. His father was a recently retired attorney who now indulged his love of travel. His mother? The only thing Karin remembered him saying about her was that she was active in civic organizations.

All the time Karin had spent in the hospital waiting room while Aaron was in the intensive care unit, she couldn't remember either parent visiting him.

This didn't necessarily mean that Aaron and his parents were estranged. Perhaps they'd been on one of their many trips. Still, no matter what reason Karin came up with for them not being at their son's side, she couldn't fail to conclude that they weren't close.

Speculations were a waste of time. At least where Aaron's private life was concerned. He would tell her about it eventually. Time was better spent directing her speculations toward Two-Point.

Karin reached for the Yellow Pages. The section of real estate agencies was discouragingly long. The woman had said the agency who'd bought the house sounded like "Sun" or "Sunny." Studying the listings for the esses, she came up with a number of possibilities: Sunnyside, Sung, Sonnfeld, and Sonnell realties. How could she find out which of these agencies had been buying up properties in the arson-struck area?

Buying. Selling. Records. Titles. That was it! She knew just the person who could help her. With a pleased smile, she reached for the phone.

Using his desk to shield him from Molly's motherly eyes, Aaron massaged his legs. Ever since he'd started the intensive physical therapy sessions, he was experiencing "discomfort" as his doctor called it. Personally, he thought what he felt was pain. Considerable pain. Aaron poured water from the carafe on his desk and downed two aspirins. Hopefully, they'd dull the pain enough to keep him from snapping at everyone in sight.

Actually, he almost welcomed the pain since it was a sign that his near-atrophied muscles responded to the grueling movements he put them through. Once they were strong enough he would be able to stand and then . . . He always thought of Karin when he envisioned himself getting out of the wheelchair. That wasn't the only time. Lately he'd had a hard time *not* thinking about her.

He couldn't believe how quickly, how completely, she'd slipped into his awareness. Even more quickly, she'd become part of his daily life at home. He could no longer imagine getting up in the morning and not finding her in the kitchen, drinking her second cup of coffee and offering him some wholesome breakfast she'd fixed. He was even acquiring a taste for oatmeal. With a shrug of his shoulders, he maneuvered the wheelchair toward the squad room.

She had wanted him to kiss her again. He'd sensed it. Thinking of how she'd looked at him, focusing those beautiful blue-green eyes on his mouth until he could almost feel her lips on his, he felt desire rip through him again. She seemed not to mind him being a cripple. He didn't understand that. In the face of his past experiences that ought to be impossible. Yet, for Karin it didn't seem to be. He shook his head in disbelieving wonder.

When he reached the open door of the squad room, he heard her warm laughter. Half-turned away from the door, she was talking to someone on the phone, her strong, muscular body relaxed in the chair, her long legs crossed.

Karin's self-restraint on the job was one of the things he liked about her. One of the many things he liked about her. Liked? What a weak word to describe his feelings for her. Aaron was careful not to analyze those feelings. This wasn't the time or the place for it. He wasn't ready to face them, but he did acknowledge that they were powerful and pervasive. Very pervasive. For the first time in his life he had trouble keeping his mind on business.

A spasm of pain in his lower right leg reminded him that he was still chained to the blasted chair he was sitting in and had no business indulging in sweet dreams. Aaron gritted his teeth. The blasted pills weren't kicking in.

He became aware of Karin's words. One especially caught his attention. Was that which he'd been so afraid of happening? Was another man winning Karin before he had a chance to woo her? Blast and triple blast this wheelchair. With a grim expression Aaron wheeled himself to Karin's desk. When she saw him, she hung up with a quick good-bye. Did she look guilty or was it his imagination that made her look so?

"Talking to your *friend* Jason again?" he asked, his voice cool. When he realized how he sounded, he apologized. "I'm sorry. That's none of my business."

"Actually it is. This wasn't a personal call. He's just the man to help us."

"And how can he do that?"

"By checking title transfers of properties in Two-Point's target area."

Karin looked mighty pleased and she had every right to be, Aaron admitted. It had been a brilliant idea to check title transfers. He'd have to curb his jealous suspicions because that's what they were. He hated to admit that he was jealous, but he was. He wanted Karin too much, yet was in no position to pursue her.

"Good job. How soon will he get back to you?"

"He said he'd look up the information first chance he got." Karin hadn't failed to hear the sarcastic note in Aaron's voice when he uttered the word 'friend'. It was time to set him straight once and for all. "My *friend* Jason, and he is my *friend*, is dating my *friend* Alice which makes me happy. It's time he stopped mourning his fiancée and got on with his life. So you can stop ragging me about him."

Chastened, Aaron said, "Consider it done."

"Good. Now, are we on for the stakeout tonight?"

"Yes."

"Before that I should go and see Crawford again. Do I have your permission to go alone?"

"No. I'll go with you."

"But it's not dangerous—" Karin broke off when she saw Aaron's forbidding expression. "Oh, all right."

"I love it when you're agreeable and docile." Aaron had the feeling she wanted to stick her tongue out at him, but settled for a squinty-eyed look. He grinned at her. To his delight, she grinned back before preceding him out the door.

Stopped at a traffic light on the way back to the office after the interview, Karin said, "Crawford was lying." She looked in the rearview mirror for Aaron's confirmation of her statement.

"He was. And he was scared."

"I bet he's on the phone right now, talking to whoever wants to buy the warehouse. If only we could have tapped his phone."

"There isn't a judge in Chicago who'd give us permission to do that with what we've got on Crawford. Which amounts to little more than suspicion based on a pattern and on instinct."

"Still, he put pressure on his tenants to give up their lease which he couldn't deny since they had consulted their attorney. That gives him motive. I don't believe that somebody offered him more money to rent the warehouse as he claimed. I bet somebody offered to buy it. He couldn't sell it as long as the warehouse was leased and since the buyer was interested in the land only, why not burn it? No problem."

"Wrong! He does have a problem. Us. We threw a scare into him today which he deserved. From what you told me, the Vietnamese family works long hours. Somebody could have been in the warehouse when it went up in flames. As soon as we get the first bit of concrete evidence, we're going back to see Crawford."

"Lean on him." Karen nodded enthusiastically.

"Where did you pick up that expression?" Aaron asked, suppressing a chuckle. The phrase was so at odds with Karen's gentle nature that it was comical.

"From Simon. I guess it's cop talk," she said, looking sheepish.

"Speaking of cops, when was the last time you qualified on the shooting range?"

Surprised, Karin sought his gaze in the rearview mirror. "A couple of months ago. Before I applied for this job. I knew that a shooting proficiency was a prerequisite. Why do you ask?"

"You and I are trained smokies rather than cops, so we're the only ones on the team who don't carry a weapon. When we're engaged in field work at arson sites I don't think we need firearms, but on stakeout duty we do. We'll carry our guns tonight. Does that make you feel uncomfortable?"

"No. I'm not crazy about guns, but I can handle one if I have to."

"Good."

"You think there could be danger?"

"Maybe. Two-Point is a pro. He's making a hell of a good living setting fires in that neighborhood. He won't be happy if someone screws that up for him. Or tries to put him behind bars. Besides, that's a rough neighborhood to be in after dark."

"Especially for a woman, right?"

"I didn't say that, but yes, a woman runs extra risks. Even a tall, strong one like you."

Aaron was quoting her earlier words. Karin couldn't help but grin. When their glances met, she saw the warm glow in his eyes that always kindled a small flame deep inside her. Was he weakening in his resolve to ignore his attraction to her? Was she winning this crucial battle? Joy bubbled through Karin, making it difficult to sit still. She wanted to turn the radio dial until she found hot, screaming guitars and pounding drums that echoed the fast beat of her heart. She couldn't do that. Their radio was set to receive reports of fires all over Chicago.

"I want you to go to the shooting range after work. Just to refresh your skills," Aaron added, catching her frowning expression.

"I'm not going to shoot myself in the foot. Or anyone else."

"I didn't think you would, but practice is always good."

"Are you going?"

"No. I have a therapy session."

"In that case, we'll eat a little later tonight." Like any wife, Karin reflected, her mind focused on household duties. Except she wasn't Aaron's wife. That was a long way off, if it ever was going to happen. True, Aaron was weakening, but with a strong-willed man like him that process was only slightly faster than the erosion of a single raindrop falling on a rock.

Still, she was making headway. She would have to bide her time. Being with him twenty-four hours a day made that extremely difficult. Their togetherness was playing havoc with her mind and her emotions.

"You're preoccupied. Are you sure carrying a gun isn't worrying you?" he asked.

His solicitousness touched her, even though it was misplaced. What would his reaction be if he knew what she'd been dreaming about? Aaron would undoubtedly be surprised if he knew how constantly he occupied her thoughts. She surprised herself. For a woman who'd vowed to keep a professional distance, she was failing miserably.

"Karin?"

She did so love the way he said her name. She forced herself back to reality. Quickly, she said, "I'm not worried about the gun. I was trying to decide what would be the fastest thing I could fix for dinner," she improvised.

"Why don't we send out for something? Chinese or pizza?"

"I get to choose?"

"You make it sound as though I always do the choosing." Aaron laid his hand on his heart with an exaggerated expression of hurt feelings. "You wound me, Karin."

"Yeah, right." Karin shot him a disapproving look which was undermined by the smile pulling on the corners of her mouth. "I'm taking you up on your offer. We'll have Chinese."

"Are you sure?"

"Absolutely, and don't try to change my mind. You picked pizza the last three times we ordered carryout food. Stir fried veggies and rice. You can have chicken or beef or shrimp with yours," Karin said, her tone magnanimous, her smile warm, her eyes loving.

Chapter Ten

At dusk, Karin drove the van slowly through the targeted four-block area, Aaron sitting at his customary spot behind her. The other investigators, dressed casually to fit the scene, patrolled the neighborhood on foot.

"You watch the left side of the street. I'll watch the right," Aaron instructed.

Karin nodded. Her eyes darted from the pavement in front of her to the sidewalk, the houses, and back to the street. It was almost completely dark now, but there was still a lot of activity in the street. The heat drove people out of their airless houses.

After circling the area twice, Aaron told Karin to park east of the railroad tracks.

"Climb into the back seat with me." When he caught Karin's surprised stare, he added, "I want you back here because the windows are tinted. The van will look like just another parked vehicle."

She sat on the one seat that hadn't been removed to make room for Aaron's wheelchair. The minutes dragged by in slow silence. They watched the street. At fifteen-minute intervals the men reported in on the walkie-talkies. All the reports were negative. By 11:00, the temperature had dropped a few degrees and the street had emptied somewhat.

"I don't think Two-Point is working tonight. If he'd planned to set a fire tonight, wouldn't he have arrived when the streets were full of people and he wouldn't be noticed so easily?" Karin asked.

"Not necessarily. True, if fewer people are out, he might stand out more, but there are also fewer pairs of eyes to see him. It works both ways. We'll stay a while longer."

Karin tried to suppress a sigh. Apparently, she didn't succeed.

"You're having a hard time sitting still this long, aren't you?"

"Yes. I'm surprised that you're not fidgeting. Usually patience isn't one of your strong points."

"Discipline, Karin."

"I'm beginning to hate that word."

"Why?" Aaron asked, his tone surprised.

"Because it rules you. It did so even before the accident, but now that's all you allow in your life: iron discipline. Nothing else."

"That's all I *can* allow myself right now. I thought you understood that."

"I do on one level, but—" Karin stopped, bending forward for a better look out the window. "Aaron, look at that van approaching us. Remember the reports of a dark-colored van in the area of the first fires? Darn!" Karin leaped from the van, squinting after the car that had just passed them. Ducking down and using the parked cars as cover, she sprinted down the sidewalk.

"Karin!"

She ignored Aaron's voice and kept running. When the van reached the corner and halted at the stop sign, she straightened up and concentrated on the license plate. She repeated the numbers she had been able to see all the way back to their van.

"Of all the fool things—"

"*Sh*," she said urgently while writing on the note pad. "I got the first digits of the license plate. The taillight was out on the left side. Possibly on purpose just so it would be impossible to get the full number."

"And did you have your gun with you when you took off?" Aaron asked icily, accepting the note pad from her.

"No. It's in my purse on the seat. Aaron, I didn't have time."

From his expression, she could tell that he was upset with her. Raising the walkie-talkie, Aaron spoke to Bryan. "A dark brown van should be passing you. Follow it. Over."

"Do I stop it? Over."

"No. Just follow it. Call me as soon as you have its destination. Over."

While she listened to Aaron giving instructions to the other men, she tried to gauge just how angry he was with her. It was hard to tell, for when he chose, he could turn his handsome face into an expressionless mask. If only he weren't so overprotective because she was a woman. If Bryan had run after the van without his gun, Aaron wouldn't even have mentioned it.

They sat, tense and silent.

A few minutes later Bryan called with bad news.

"I lost him. Some jerk driving one of those rental moving trucks lost control and careened all over the street with it. By the time he got the truck under control, the brown van had disappeared. I'm sorry."

"Bad break, but it isn't your fault. I'll phone in the partial number to the DMV. Two-Point was undoubtedly casing the street. He won't be back tonight. For now, let's call it a night," Aaron instructed.

When they arrived at Aaron's house, Karin followed him into the kitchen. She watched him rummage through the 'fridge for a few seconds before she asked, "Can I help you find something?"

"Yeah. Something to eat. That Chinese food didn't stick to my ribs. I always thought that was stereotype, but it seems to be true. I'm hungry. What have we got to eat?"

"How about fruit, cheese and crackers?"

"Sounds good."

Karin set out the Camembert to let it warm slightly before she washed the fruit and put crackers on a plate. She placed the food on the kitchen table and joined Aaron there. While they ate, she studied him. Aaron looked tired. The strain around his mouth told her that he was in pain. Though she longed to comfort him, to ease the pain with a soft touch and soothing words, she forced herself to sit quietly. She had no choice. Aaron hated compassion. He mistook it for pity.

"You've been watching me like a cat watches a mouse. What's wrong? What's bothering you? Spit it out before you choke on it," he demanded, his voice challenging, his eyes narrowed.

Caught, she frantically cast about for a reasonable explanation, a rationalization, she could use. No, not again. It was time to bring the truth out into the open.

"All right. Since you asked, there are a couple of things on my mind."

"No kidding," Aaron muttered, his voice ironic.

Undaunted because she knew this was his way of throwing up protective barriers, she continued. "Yes, no kidding. Why is it okay for you to be damn protective of me, but if I look concerned about you, your hands-off signals flash a red warning? Either you stop being protective of me or let me respond in kind. Nothing less is fair or acceptable."

Stunned, Aaron merely stared at Karin for several

seconds. Finally he managed to choke out two words. "Overprotective? Me?"

"Yes, you. Tonight was a good example and it wasn't the only one. I won't bother to recite every single instance of it, but there have been plenty. If you can worry about me, I can worry about you."

Aaron ran his hand through his hair in a distracted manner. After a lengthy silence he spoke. His voice sounded resigned. "If I'm protective of you, it's because you're *you*, but I'd be protective of any woman in this line of work. Perhaps not to the same extent, though." For a moment he toyed with a grape before putting it back on his plate.

"Our work is dangerous, and whether you like it or not, women face extra risks. Not because they're less capable, but because there are guys out there who'd attack a woman when they'd think twice about challenging a man. And that's the truth."

Karin never took her eyes off Aaron. She watched him reach for a pear and start to peel it. She guessed he hoped she would be satisfied with this explanation. She wasn't, and she wasn't about to let him off the hook that easily. She simply kept looking at him silently, expectantly until he stopped peeling the pear and faced her.

"I suppose you're waiting to hear me say it, aren't you?" he ground out.

"Yes." She saw his jaws tighten and his lips compress before he forced himself to relax marginally. His voice, his expression, were controlled when he spoke.

"I'm protective of you because. . . ."

"Because. . . ." Karin prompted.

"Damn it to hell and back, woman, we used to care deeply about each other!"

Finally a small dent in his control, Karin thought, pure exhilaration surging to every cell of her body. "Yes, we did. Until you ended it."

"I had no other choice."

"Yes, you did," Karin said softly.

"Bind you to a cripple with two useless legs? That's not a choice. That's a life sentence. I wasn't about to inflict that on you."

"Not even when I was willing and eager to take you, wheelchair and all?"

"Not even then. *Especially* not then."

"That was the most selfish decision you ever made. You drove me away without considering my feelings, without asking me what I wanted. Do you have any idea how that hurt me? How guilty that made me feel?"

Aaron frowned. "Hold on. What do you mean, it made you feel guilty? Why on earth would you feel guilty?"

"Because I'd chosen that evening to discuss what was wrong with our relationship. How you didn't need me. How you shut me out emotionally. How everything else was more important to you than me. You were extremely upset when you left for that fire."

"And you thought my judgment might have been thrown off by that, that I might have been careless?" The expression in her eyes confirmed his guess. "My God, Karin, I had no idea you felt this way. Let me put your mind at ease. I wasn't careless. You know how unpredictable a fire is. You think it'll go one way and then it'll go another. What happened was an accident, pure and simple. It wasn't my fault, and it certainly wasn't yours."

"Then why wouldn't you let me help you? Why did you make sure I left that hospital convinced that it was all over between us? Do you realize how high-handed that was?"

"Karin, it was best that way. For both of us."

Her voice exploded into the tense silence of the kitchen with a fervently uttered, "Says who?"

"At that time the doctors gave me nine to one odds of ever regaining any feeling below my waist and even worse odds for me ever walking again. For all practical purposes I was doomed to be a helpless cripple." He raised his hand to forestall the passionate outburst he sensed was coming. "You say you wouldn't have minded the wheelchair. Being the kind of woman you are, you *would* say that, and probably even mean it at that moment, but soon disillusionment would have gnawed at your commitment and affection until they turned into resentment and revulsion. I saw that happen years ago, and I wasn't about to let that happen to us."

Karin raised her hands towards him. "Right now I

want nothing more than to grab your shoulders and shake you till your bones rattle! I'm that furious with you. How dare you assume I'd have acted that way? I wouldn't have," she cried out impassioned. "You keep mistaking pity for compassion. Pity might be tinged with condescension, but compassion isn't. Compassion is the sympathy, the tenderness, you feel for a person you care about. It's understanding their suffering and wanting to help, wanting to help so desperately that you'd gladly sacrifice your right arm, your eyes, your soul, to help ease their pain."

"Karin—"

"No, this time you have to let me finish." She took a shaky breath. "I know how I feel. What I don't know is why you feel the way you do about being crippled. Don't you think it's time for that long, sad story you promised to tell me?"

"Yeah, I guess maybe it is."

Aaron closed his eyes for a moment as if to prepare himself for a difficult task. Karin tensed in anticipation.

"I had a brother, Robert. He was four years younger than me."

"Robert? The sketch upstairs that's framed so nicely is his, isn't it?"

"Yes. He liked to color and he was surprisingly good at it, given the fact that he was born mentally and physically handicapped."

Aaron's bittersweet smile of remembrance, and his

soft, gentle tone spoke eloquently of the love he felt for his brother.

"Robert lived with us for the first four years of his life, but the older he got, the more pronounced his handicaps became. Finally, my parents put him into an institution."

Karin reached for Aaron's hand and squeezed it. "How awful for all of you."

"Thank you." Aaron raised her hand and pressed it against his cheek.

Karin waited for him to continue. Finally she asked, "What happened to Robert?"

"He died shortly after he was institutionalized."

Aaron's pause revealed how difficult it was for him to talk about this.

Karin fought the tears of empathy that sprang into her eyes. When she could, she murmured, "I'm sorry." Now she understood Aaron, understood his instinctive fear of being handicapped.

Where would they go from here? she wondered.

As if he sensed her question, he said, "Karin, I still have wheels for legs. Basically, nothing's changed."

"I wouldn't say that," she informed him softly. At last he had shared something of himself with her. It was a beginning. Karin moved her thumb to the corner of his lips where she paused briefly to study their beautiful shape. She felt the quick intake of his breath which thrilled her. With feather-soft strokes she moved the pad of her thumb over his mouth, never taking her eyes off it.

Aaron's breathing turned ragged. That's all the encouragement she needed. She took the initiative and kissed him tenderly.

Then she moved back, just out of reach. Both were silent, sitting quietly. Finally he said, "I better put in some time on my exercise machine if I hope to catch a few hours of sleep." Without a backward glance he wheeled himself out of the kitchen.

Karin understood that he wasn't ready to trust her not to reject him. What had happened to his brother had put the idea into his head that to be handicapped could lead to being rejected, abandoned. It would take a while longer to change his mind. If she could convince him.

She sighed. The confrontation had given her a splitting headache. Perhaps a leisurely bath would make her feel better, Karin thought, slowly walking upstairs.

Vulcan was lying in the middle of her bed.

"At least you don't run away when I touch you," she said, stroking his silky fur.

She was feeling sorry for herself, Karin realized, appalled. It was one emotion she had no use for. She'd brought home the file on Two-Point. She would study it, she resolved. Work always made her feel better.

Two minutes after 9:00 the next morning, the DMV telephoned them at the office. Three minutes later, Aaron called to Karin to grab her purse and get a move on. He grinned when she almost leaped over her desk to join him. He did adore her enthusiasm. Among other things. Many other things.

He had studied her lovely face closely at breakfast. His relief had been heartfelt when he realized that she was determined to continue the status quo. He was also immensely grateful that she hadn't referred to their conversation of the night before. Outside of his immediate family, no one knew of Robert and of that painful part of his life. He had never told anyone about his brother. Odd, that he'd been able to confide in Karin. Odder still, that it felt so right that he had. What was it about her that got to him on levels no other woman had ever reached?

How had she penetrated his protective walls so quickly? She hadn't just penetrated them. Karin had burned them down as if they'd been made of papier-mâché. He thought of the nickname his students had given him and shook his head. Some Iron Knight he turned out to be. More like a flimsy, paper-thin tin man, melted by the fire of one woman. His woman.

When had he started thinking about Karin as his woman? He couldn't remember, but this possessive term must have simmered just under his awareness. He'd have to watch himself. He couldn't, wouldn't make her his woman until he could get out of that confounded wheelchair.

When they were seated in the van, she asked, "Where to?"

"Evanston."

She couldn't hide her surprise. "I hadn't pictured Two-Point living in a university town. At least that's how I think of Evanston."

"The owner of the brown van isn't necessarily our arsonist."

"True. He—" she paused to glance at Aaron over her shoulder. "Is it a he?" Karin asked.

"Yes." Aaron consulted the piece of paper in his hand. "Thomas Williams. He could be in on the arson. He could get a cut of the fee. Or he could be totally unaware of how his van was used."

"I take it the van wasn't reported stolen?" Karin asked.

"No."

The address was not in the better part of town. The house was in poor condition, as was its elderly owner. Thomas Williams moved slowly, cumbersomely, with the aid of a metal walker. Politely they listened to his account of the hip operation which had prevented him from driving the van for the last three months. He admitted freely that his sister, Mary Ann Gingrich, often borrowed the van. Karin and Aaron exchanged a meaningful look.

"Do your sister's children drive the van?" Karin asked.

"She's got only one. I told her I didn't want Leo driving the van."

"Why's that Mr. Williams?" Karin asked.

"Because he's a wrong 'n. Probably not all his fault. Mary Ann spoiled him rotten."

His face assumed a closed expression. Aaron realized they'd get nothing more from the old man. After thanking him, they left. Using the cell phone, Aaron issued a series of orders, ranging from getting Mrs. Gingrich's address, to checking Leo for prior convictions, to surveillance of both the Williams and the Gingrich residences.

"We're moving," Aaron said, his voice vibrating with satisfaction. "Let's head back."

At the office, Molly handed Karin a message from Jason. Both Sonnell and Sunnyside realties had bought several properties in Two-Point's target zone. It was now a matter of finding out which one had hired the arsonist. Perhaps she could narrow that down by studying the colored-in map in the conference room.

Karin spent a long time studying the map before she decided that Sunnyside Realty was probably not involved in whatever was going on. Before she could say with certainty that Sonnell was the company they needed to investigate, she had to check ownership of several properties in the area. Aaron was on the phone, so she told Molly where she was going.

It was late afternoon when she finished the tedious records' search. She didn't even pause at her desk but headed straight for the conference room and the map. She was busily cross-hatching some of the squares when Aaron joined her.

"That's an interesting pattern, but what does it mean?" he asked.

"Properties acquired by Sonnell Realty."

Aaron whistled, impressed.

"Interesting that they own all the properties adjacent to the recently torched buildings, isn't it?"

"Makes one wonder if they hired someone to burn out the reluctant sellers."

"But why in heaven's name would anybody want to buy up property in a neighborhood like that?" Karin asked.

"Not to restore the run-down buildings, that's for sure. Sonnell probably has a buyer lined up who'll undoubtedly raze the entire area to erect something big."

"So all we have to do is prove that they hired an arsonist. And catch him first, of course."

"We will," Aaron assured her. "Now let's go home. Tonight's the night." When he saw her look puzzled, he asked, his tone chiding, "Have you forgotten that to-night is the ladies fund-raiser we promised to attend?"

Karin groaned. "It had slipped my mind. Do we have to go?"

"We do. But we lucked out. Because of the stakeout, we have a legitimate excuse to eat and run. We'll show up for the the food, pay our respects, drop off my con-tribution, and excuse ourselves."

"That doesn't sound too bad," Karin admitted.

"I'm going to physical therapy. If you drop me off at

the clinic, Don will pick me up. That'll give you enough time to get ready."

Guiltily, she remembered that Alice had insisted on coming to Aaron's house, and here she had totally forgotten about the party. Ostensibly, Alice came to bring the hose she'd bought, but Karin suspected it was to lend a hand and make her look as glamorous as she could.

Karin studied her mirror image critically. The red dress really did something for her. Or maybe it was the elegant upswept hairdo that Alice had created for her. Or maybe it was just the exciting prospect of being with Aaron socially that lent a glow to her face and a sparkle to her eyes. Whatever it was, Karin hoped Aaron would approve of her appearance.

He was waiting for her at the bottom of the steps. She stopped for a moment to look at him. Even though she had tried to imagine him in a tuxedo, she hadn't anticipated how elegant and breathtakingly handsome the formal evening wear would look on him. Conscious that he never took his eyes off her, she forced herself to walk slowly toward him. When she reached his side, she stopped.

"That's some dress," he said, his voice husky. Aaron touched the silky material. His fingers slid over the short length of her dress to the shimmering, pale sheen of her hose. When he realized he was touching her thigh, he jerked his hand away. "You realize that this dress was designed for seduction, don't you?"

"Was it?" she asked, all wide-eyed innocence.

"You know darn well it was," he growled. "Let's go."

Even though they arrived early, there was already a long line in front of the serving table. When her mother saw them, she abandoned her post and came to greet them.

"Darling, you look great. I love the dress." Then she turned her attention to Karin's escort. "Hello, Aaron. Nice to see you again. Come, I have a place reserved for you right over here," she said, proceeding to fuss over Aaron like a mother hen.

He endured the solicitous attentions with remarkable grace and charm which obviously captured Hedwig Bergstrom. Her mother never had a chance, Karin mused. But then neither had she. Aaron had attracted her from the moment she first saw him, and he had captured her heart a ridiculously short time later.

Her mother served them personally and hovered over them when Aaron confided that they had to leave early because of a case they were working on. Amazed, Karin eyed the huge portions her mother had heaped on his plate. Aaron grinned at her before digging in with obvious enjoyment.

Chief Edwards joined them briefly. Aaron brought him up to date on the case. The chief wished them good luck in catching Two-Point and asked to be kept informed of their progress. He smiled at Karin approvingly before he rejoined his party.

To Aaron's delight, Karin's mother wrapped a couple of pieces of her blackberry pie for an after stakeout snack. Hugging Karin good-bye, Mrs. Bergstrom murmured, "You really do look lovely, honey. Aren't you glad you took my advice and bought a sexy dress? I think Aaron's wonderful. He reminds me of your father, rest his soul."

Deep down, Karin was pleased by her mother's approval of Aaron. And Aaron did share the quiet strength, the inborn integrity, the natural courage, that had characterized her father. She mused on the similarities all the way home where they changed clothes and left for the stakeout.

No sooner had they reached their destination, when one of those horrendous summer thunderstorms pummeled the city. They sat through the storm and the steady rain that followed until after midnight when Aaron called it a night.

Chapter Eleven

After the previous night's thunderstorm, the heat wave descended on the city again with a vengeance. It was still hot and humid when the team headed for the stakeout that evening.

Once in position, the men reported in at regular intervals.

"Two-Point is taking the Garfield Exit, heading in your direction." Simon's voice crackled with excitement as he reported the suspected arsonist's location on his cell phone.

Using a walkie-talkie, Aaron related the message to the investigators who were moving through the neighborhood around the two possible target buildings.

This is it, Karin thought, wiping her sweating palms on her jeans.

"He's heading for the duplex," Simon informed them.

Without a word, Karin pointed the van in the direction of the two-family house.

They saw the brown van stop across the street from the duplex, but Two-Point didn't get out. They waited.

"What's he up to?" Karin wondered out loud.

"Let's find out. Drive past him," Aaron said.

Karin did. When she passed the empty lot next to the targeted house, they saw the reason for the arsonist's hesitation.

"What on earth?" Aaron muttered, adding a couple of swear words. He picked up the walkie-talkie. "Everybody hold your position. Looks like a bunch of teenagers built a bonfire in the empty lot next to the duplex. We'll park in the alley down the block and keep an eye on the suspect."

Karin pulled into the alley. Only then did they discover that it had been blocked off with discarded furniture and the hulk of an abandoned car. Knowing how important it was to position their vehicle ready to take off in seconds, she asked, "Since I can't turn around in here, do you want me to back out and then back into the alley?"

"No, that might draw Gingrich's attention. Lower the platform. We'll watch from the entrance to the alley. I'll alert Simon to be ready to take up pursuit should it become necessary."

That's what they did. Far enough back to be hidden

in the shadow of the building but close enough to keep Two Point's van in sight, they watched and waited. From their hiding place they couldn't see the bonfire, but they heard the teenagers' laughter and the music from a boom box.

"Sounds like they're having a good time," Karin murmured, wiping perspiration from her neck.

"Yeah, we might be here most of the night. If Two-Point's smart, he'll wait them out and use the bonfire to make it look like the cause of the duplex going up in flames."

Ten minutes later, they heard sirens. When they came closer and closer, Aaron cursed volubly. "Somebody called the cops to break up the kids' party."

Sure enough, seconds later two patrol cars, lights flashing and sirens blasting, pulled up to the bonfire. While the cops were busy with the kids, Two-Point started the van and drove off.

The walkie-talkie crackled into life. "Aaron, do you want me to follow him?" Simon asked.

"Yes, and report back. Everyone else stay put. He might be back as soon as the squad cars leave."

Again they waited. With the teenagers dispersed and the squad cars gone, the neighborhood quieted down considerably. Simon informed them that Two-Point was going north on the expressway.

"He's too cautious to try again tonight. We might as well go home." Aaron waited until all the men had been dismissed before they turned toward the van. They never reached it.

Out of the shadows a figure leaped at Aaron. Before either of them could react, the man had placed a hammer lock around Aaron and a second attacker faced Karin with a long, wicked-looking knife. It all happened within a couple of seconds.

"Lady, empty your purse," the knife-wielding man ordered.

Recovering from the shock of the attack, Karin managed to say, "All right." Slowly, she slid her shoulder bag down her left arm, weighing their options. The chances that the men would let them leave unharmed were slim. This was their territory. They held the upper hand. When the bag reached the crook of her arm, Karin grabbed it and flung it at her attacker. With her right hand she reached for the gun she carried in a her newly acquired holster at the small of her back.

"Freeze," she yelled, crouching down into the classical shooter's stance.

When the man holding Aaron was momentarily distracted by Karin's move, Aaron took advantage of that and freed himself from the man's grip. In the process, both men fell to the ground.

Alarmed, Karin called out to Aaron and rushed toward him. She knew this gave the men a chance to escape, but she didn't care. Aaron was more important than a pair of muggers. When she tried to help him back into the wheelchair, he told her to back off. He didn't need her help. He struggled to hoist himself into his chair before speaking.

"Damn it to hell and back, Karin, you let them get away," he yelled.

"I thought you might be hurt."

Angrily, he shook off the hand she'd laid on his arm. Without looking at her he wheeled himself into the van.

Karin followed. "Shall I report this attempted mugging to the nearest precinct?"

"And tell them what? That I lay helplessly on the ground? That my assistant was too concerned about her crippled boss to detain the muggers? The cops'll get a real kick out of that. Besides, neither of us can give any kind of description of the muggers since it was too dark to see anything more than the outline of their bodies."

He was far angrier than she had anticipated. Wisely, she refrained from saying anything else until they entered the kitchen of his house. She waited until Aaron had poured himself a glass of orange juice. Then she said, "Let's talk about it."

"What's to talk about? Between your concern and my physical disability, we let two criminals get away."

The bitterness of his voice chilled her. Softly, she said, "Those two lowlifes will get caught sooner or later. I thought your welfare was more important than they were. I still think so."

"You're not supposed to think that. The job comes first."

"I disagree. Moreover, I don't believe you really buy that either, not when you have this ironclad rule about partners protecting each other. Aaron, what's really bothering you?" she demanded. "What's this really about?"

"It's about me sitting like a lump on a log while you face two muggers, that's what this is about. How do you think I felt, eating dirt on the ground, helpless to do anything while you had to pull a gun on those scumballs? Lower than a worm. That's how!" Aaron brought his fists down forcefully on top of his thighs. "Useless, helpless cripple!" He whipped his chair around and rapidly left the kitchen.

Karin raised her hand to her mouth to contain the sobs that rose in her throat. The disciplined mask Aaron usually wore had finally slipped. For the first time Karin had seen the naked anguish and the desperation she'd only sensed in him before. It filled her heart with searing pain.

Karin awoke just before dawn. As quietly as she could, she went to the kitchen and brewed a pot of extra-strength coffee.

When he heard her, Aaron gave up any pretense of resting and joined her in the kitchen. Her lovely face looked pale, worn. She obviously hadn't slept much either. Guiltily he wondered if she'd been crying. The last thing on earth he wanted to do was hurt her. Yet he obviously had done just that. Again.

"Aaron, do you want a cup of coffee?"

"Yes, please." Never taking his eyes off her, Aaron watched Karin fill his mug and place it on the table in front of him. She was close enough that he caught her early morning scent—that clean combination of soap, shampoo, and lotion. He identified each element: citrus, spring flowers, lily of the valley . . . and Karin. A heady mix. Appealing. Unforgettable. Just like her.

If he lived to be a hundred, he would never forget how she had looked, facing the two muggers. Like a Viking warrior queen—proud, unafraid to take them on single-handedly. And that was his shameful problem. That she'd had to take them on alone while he lay helpless on the ground. A man was supposed to protect his—Unable to complete the thought, Aaron gripped the wheels of his chair. The hard rubber dug into his palms, reminding him that he still needed those wheels. And as long as he did, he had no right to Karin. It was as simple as that.

Forcing himself to let go of the wheels, Aaron took a sip of coffee.

"Would you like some breakfast?"

"No, thank you." Aaron tried to gauge Karin's mood. She seemed quietly determined to carry on as if nothing out of the ordinary had happened. Aaron, though, couldn't dismiss the previous night quite so easily.

"You got your wish last night." Seeing her surprised look, he added, "You saw my supposedly tenacious discipline break down. Some 'Iron Knight' I turned out to be. More like one made out of papier-mâché."

"Or out of flesh and blood, like the rest of us?"

Karin would think that, Aaron thought, warmth rushing through him like a healing balm. She didn't despise him. He felt the tightness around his chest snap. *Don't let go yet. You're still in this chair.*

The ringing of the telephone gave him a chance to pull himself together.

"Yes, he's here. Just a moment, please." Karin handed the receiver to Aaron.

She saw the old fighting spirit take hold of Aaron as he listened. Thank God.

Hanging up, he said, "Leo Gingrich, or Two-Point as we call him, served time for assault. Guess what his cell mate was in for?"

"Arson?"

"Exactly."

"I was only guessing!" Karin exclaimed.

"That's where he learned his new trade."

"Whatever doubts we had that he was Two-Point, are now wiped out. Still, we need proof. For the courts."

"We'll get it. Better still, we'll catch him in the act." Aaron's voice was filled with absolute certainty. "Ready to go to work?"

"Absolutely."

At the office, Karin and Simon waited calmly for Aaron to get off the phone. While Karin studied arson statistics in their district, Simon read the *Tribune*. After a few minutes, he said, "Hmm. Alderman Rezlab is promising the South Side residents again that they'll get a new industrial complex which will provide hundreds of new jobs. What a liar! Where will he get the space?"

Karin almost didn't catch the implication of Simon's remark. "Wait a minute. How large an area would they need for an industrial park?"

"Oh, I don't know. Several square blocks at least."

Aaron put the phone down. "Read Alderman Rezlab's statement again," he requested.

Simon did. When he finished, he looked in astonishment from Aaron to Karin. "Could he be referring to our torched area as the new site?"

"It's possible," Aaron said, tapping a pencil against the desk top. "We know Sonnell Realty wants that land. Karin, can you find out who owns the real estate agency?"

"Yes. I should be able to get a list of the executive board members. I wonder how the alderman is connected to the agency," she murmured.

"I'd like to know that, too," Aaron said.

"Jeez, if he is, what a stink that'll raise!" Simon said. Then, philosophically, he added, "But politicians have done favors for friends and business acquaintances before. For the right fee, of course."

Karin consulted all sources known to her. This included a phone call to Jason, who talked for five minutes about how wonderful Alice was. With a smile,

Karin listened to him. After he promised to get her the information she needed before the day was over, she headed to the reference section of the main branch of the public library.

It was late afternoon before she returned to the office. Aaron had just come back from his physical therapy session. He looked worn out, she thought, but kept herself from commenting on that. After last night, he would be more determined than ever to get out of that wheelchair.

"Did you find out anything about Sonnell Realty?" he asked.

"Did I ever! For about five minutes, I was convinced that I'd discovered a dummy corporation." Karin scooted around the desk so Aaron could see the diagram she'd drawn. "Sonnell Realty is owned by Crossbow, Inc. which in turn is a subsidiary of Kinad Construction."

"That's a big company. I've seen their signs all over town," Aaron said.

"They've been quite successful in their bids for city projects."

They exchanged a look, both wondering if Kinad's low bids had all been due to clever planning and a sharp pencil, or if they'd had inside tips prior to submission.

"I'm waiting for information on one of the junior officers of the company. Remember the banquet I went to with Jason?" When Aaron nodded, she continued, "Alderman Rezlab spoke at the dinner. He also introduced his extended family. I think I heard a name there that I saw listed on the roster of Kinad's executives."

"When will you get the information?"

"Before we go home." Karin glanced at her watch. "Within the hour. Do you think Two-Point will try again tonight?"

"Probably. The surveillance team reports that he appears to be unaware of our interest in him, so there's no reason he shouldn't try again."

While Karin gathered her notes, Aaron watched her. She looked breathtakingly lovely, he thought, in a matching slacks and blouse outfit in an off-white shade.

"I better go and finish some of my reports," Karin said.

For an instant Aaron was tempted to ask her to stay, to keep him company. He decided against it. It was better to focus on work.

The evening stakeout started out as a repetition of the previous surveillances. Knowing that the alley was blocked, Karin backed into it. They sat and waited. When the phone rang, Karin jumped. Her nerves were taut with anticipation.

Aaron picked up the phone. After a moment he handed it to Karin. "For you. It's Jason."

Karin accepted Jason's apologies for not getting back to her sooner, but he'd run into a slight snag before he'd gotten the information she needed. Thanking him, Karin hung up.

"I was right. The name I heard at the banquet is the same that appears on the roster of Kinad Construction. Alderman Rezlab's son-in-law is a vice president at Kinad."

"Bingo."

"Do you think we'll ever prove the connection between the Alderman, Kinad, Sonnell and Two-Point's fires?" Karin asked.

"It won't be easy, not unless we can persuade Two-Point to tell us who hired him." Seeing her worried expression, Aaron squeezed Karin's hand.

That was the first time he'd touched her since the unfortunate encounter with the muggers. His hand on hers felt so good, so right. Remembering her heart-stopping panic when that mugger had grabbed Aaron, Karin shuddered. In that instant she'd admitted to herself how deeply she felt about Aaron. Odd, how the possibility of death stripped away all rationalizations, all pretenses and left nothing but the naked truth.

Remembering the truth, Karin entwined her fingers with Aaron's. When he didn't object, she released the breath she'd been holding. Sitting in the darkness of the summer night, she heard snatches of music, children's voices, a woman's laughter, the barking of a dog. She heard Aaron's breathing and her own heartbeat. She felt strangely happy. With a wry smile which the darkness hid, she admitted that it didn't take much to make her happy. Just Aaron sitting beside her, holding her hand, filled her heart with unutterable joy.

At 9:00, Simon reported that Two-Point had left the house and was heading south. He kept them appraised of the suspect's progress.

Aaron, who'd arranged for a patrol car to pick up the residents of the house should it look as if Two-Point might strike that night, put the call through to the precinct. Ten minutes later they watched an unmarked police car take the inhabitants away.

Excitement was building as the arsonist came closer and closer. Karin found it difficult to remain seated, waiting quietly. Only Aaron's hand on her shoulder kept her still.

They watched the brown van circle the block once before its driver parked it on the lot where the teens had built the bonfire the night before.

Aaron instructed Bryan to station himself across the street and advise them of Two-Point's activities.

"He's walking around the outside of the house," Bryan said.

After a minute or two, he added, "I'll be darned. He's got the front door open and is going in, as brazen as a seasoned streetwalker meeting the incoming fleet."

Karin grinned at the colorful simile.

"Nobody try to stop him yet. We need to catch him in the act. Remember, we've got a fire truck standing by," Aaron said.

They waited for a small eternity, or so it seemed to Karin. In reality, it was only minutes.

"He's coming back out and going to the van." After a short silence Bryan added, "He's carrying a big box. Any bets on what's in it?"

Aaron checked his watch. "It shouldn't take him longer than ten minutes to set the fire," he said to Karin.

She tried not to look at her watch right away. When she did she was dismayed to see that only four minutes had elapsed. Aaron reached out to squeeze her arm.

"Take it easy. We'll get him. We know where he lives should he get away from us here."

"Here he comes, minus the box," Bryan said, his voice trembling with excitement.

"Go to your assigned stations now," Aaron ordered into the walkie-talkie.

That meant that Bryan would apprehend Gingrich. Just in case he needed help, both Karin and Aaron started toward the empty lot. They were in time to see Gingrich raise an object and bring it down forcefully on Bryan's head. The investigator fell to the ground. The arsonist ran toward the back.

"The suspect's running south across the lot," Aaron informed the team via the walkie-talkie. "Karin, help Bryan."

Rapidly, Aaron wheeled himself back toward the alley while Karin rushed to see how badly hurt Bryan was.

When she reached him, the investigator sat up, clutching his head.

"He clonked me with his metal flashlight," he muttered.

Karin helped him up. "Lean on me. We've got a first aid kit in the van. You're bleeding."

Though he was hurt, Bryan moved remarkably fast, Karin thought. When they reached the van, she became aware of the fight taking place farther back in the alley.

"Aaron," she whispered. Fear stopped her heartbeat for a count before it resumed beating in double time. Speechlessly she watched Aaron hurl himself at Two-Point and wrestle him to the ground. Bryan wanted to rush to Aaron's aid, but Karin stopped him. "No, it's important that Aaron do this himself." Even though she knew that this was Aaron's fight, it didn't stop her from slipping the gun out of the holster and holding it behind her back. She wasn't about to stand by idly while the man she loved got hurt.

It wasn't much of a fight. Aaron twisted the man's arms behind his back and slapped handcuffs on his wrists. Aaron's face was bathed in sweat from the effort.

"Bryan, how about reading him his rights," Aaron said, pointing to the arsonist.

Clamping a piece of gauze against his head, Bryan said, "I'll be only too happy to take care of that." When he passed Aaron, the investigator said, "Great tackle, boss."

Surreptitiously, Karin holstered her gun. She forced herself to remain where she was. The night before

Aaron had rejected her help. It was up to him to make the first move.

"I need your help," Aaron said quietly to Karin.

She was beside him in a flash. Speaking so low that only he could hear her, she said, "This is the first time you've ever said you needed me."

"I know, but it won't be the last."

Their eyes met and held. In the background they heard Bryan read the Miranda statement. With a tremulous smile, Karin placed her arm around Aaron's waist and helped him back into the wheelchair.

Bryan finished reading the rights to Two-Point. "Now what, boss?" he asked.

"Take him and book him for attempted arson and three counts of arson."

"Not so fast," Gingrich said. "How about cutting me a deal?"

"What kind of a deal?" Aaron asked.

"A reduced charge. The State's Attorney is always interested in plea bargaining."

"Depends on what you have to bargain with."

"I might remember who hired me," the arsonist said.

Aaron nodded. "I'll inform the prosecutor."

Loud, happy voices filled the conference room. Karin watched the investigators who'd participated in the successful stake out. They were laughing, joking, eating pizza, drinking cans of pop, exuding that indescribable high that a successfully completed case aroused.

Aaron and she hadn't had a moment alone together since they'd nabbed Two-Point. Every so often their eyes met, his filled with a golden warmth that was more precious than sunshine to her. Soon, she hoped, all these men would go home and then she and Aaron— What? Karin didn't know what would happen between them. She toyed with the same piece of cold pizza that she was too nervous to eat.

Not joining the men in this celebratory session had been unthinkable. Yet, as the minutes turned into an hour, Aaron couldn't help but wish that they'd all go home soon. In the meantime, he tried to keep his eyes off Karin, but increasingly he found that impossible to do. In honor of the stakeout, she'd worn a black tee shirt which showed off her fair coloring, and black jeans which hugged her body as if designed specifically for her. She stirred his blood mightily.

Finally, the last slice of pizza devoured, the last can of soda drained, the men headed for the door. Aaron accompanied them. He shook hands, thanked them, and congratulated each on a job well done.

Karin dumped the empty cartons, cans and paper napkins into the trash to give herself something to do. She couldn't believe how nervous she was. What would Aaron say when he came back?

"I thought they'd never leave," Aaron said, reentering the room.

A hope-inspiring statement, Karin decided. "They had to let off a little steam." She smiled at him.

What a smile. It pierced Aaron's heart with the force of a flame thrower. How had she penetrated his protective walls so quickly, so completely? She hadn't merely penetrated them. She had incinerated them. He took a deep breath. Time for the truth.

"Karin, you said you didn't mind my being in this wheelchair," he began, his voice somewhat tentative.

"I said that, and I meant it." Sensing how hard this was for Aaron, Karin walked to him. Dropping to her knees in front of him, she placed her hands on his thighs. She gazed at him, her eyes brimming with love.

"When you look at me like that, I can almost believe in miracles. I *can* believe you."

"Believe me," she murmured. "I don't love your legs or just one part of you. I love all that is you. Remember the axiom about the whole being greater than any of its parts? That's how love is: all inclusive, all powerful, all eternal."

Aaron's voice shook with wonder when he asked, "Is that how you love me?"

"Yes."

"Oh, Karin." With a groan he pulled her into his lap. Cradling her against his heart, he fought to control the emotions that tore at him. When he could, he spoke. "I wanted to believe that you loved me no matter what, but I was afraid to. I thought it might have been only pity that brought you to me in the hospital. That would have killed me. So it was easier to send you away, even though it was the hardest thing I've ever done. Or ever will do."

Karin looked deeply into his eyes. She saw the truth there. "Now do you believe me that your wheelchair doesn't bother me? Doesn't repel me?"

"Yes. I love you, Karin. I loved you before the accident even though I never said the words. I never stopped loving you. I only told myself that I did because that's the only way I could go on. And I do need you. Oh, how I need you."

Karin pressed closer, burying her lips against his warm neck.

Aaron felt her tears against his neck. "Oh, Karin, my sweet, sweet Karin."

"This is crazy. I'm so happy I can't stop crying."

Gently, tenderly he kissed the tears from her cheeks, her eyes. Only then did he claim her lips. Aaron didn't have to wait for a response. The kiss immediately heated, deepened. It was like a tiny ember receiving a blast of pure oxygen. It roared into a blaze. Pleasure spread like wildfire through his body, his brain. A strong tremor shook him. Breathless, he released her.

"Will you come home with me, Karin?"

Understanding what he was asking her, she nodded, her heart hammering with excitement and happiness. She had to take a couple of breaths before she could speak. "Should I resign as your assistant?"

"No, not unless you want to. As I told you, you have a job until another position opens up." A grin spread across his face. "Come to think of it, I have heard of another position that I hope will appeal to you. It offers room and board, half my income, and all of my love. Will you marry me?"

"Oh, yes."

They kissed, sealing their pledge.

Considerably later, and out of breath, Aaron said, "I have a surprise for you. But in order to show it to you, you'll have to get off my lap."

"I rather like being on your lap," Karin murmured.

"And I rather love having you on my lap, but you'll like this surprise."

Karin slid off his lap and stepped back expectantly. She watched him place his feet on the ground, watched him hoist himself up out of the wheelchair. He stood before her, tall and proud, smiling broadly.

"I've been practicing. I didn't tell you right away because I was afraid it might be a fluke. But it isn't. I've been able to stand on my own legs four times now. All that extra therapy paid off."

Karin blinked back tears of wonder and gratitude. "I always knew you could do it," she murmured. "It wasn't an accident that the students called you the Iron Knight." With a smile she added, "And now you're my Iron Knight."

Their eyes met and held, wordlessly conveying their feelings. Their love, risen from the ashes, was soaring like flames fueled by a wild, wild wind.